Readers love *There Has to Be a Reason*
by KATE MCMURRAY

"…a beautifully written story. Very
realistic. Definitely a book I would
recommend to others."
—Gay Book Reviews

"…I really enjoyed this. I had never
read this author before but will
definitely read more of her work."
—Night Owl Reviews

"This was a great angsty coming of
age story."
—Alpha Book Club

By KATE MCMURRAY

Blind Items
The Boy Next Door
Devin December
Four Corners
Kindling Fire with Snow
Out in the Field
Playing Ball (Multiple Author Anthology)
The Stars that Tremble • The Silence of the Stars
A Walk in the Dark
What There Is
When the Planets Align

DREAMSPUN DESIRES
#14 – The Greek Tycoon's Green Card Groom

THE RAINBOW LEAGUE
The Windup
Thrown a Curve
The Long Slide Home

WMU
There Has to Be a Reason
What's the Use of Wondering

Published by DREAMSPINNER PRESS
www.dreamspinnerpress.com

WHAT'S THE USE OF WONDERING?

KATE McMURRAY

Published by

DREAMSPINNER PRESS

5032 Capital Circle SW, Suite 2, PMB# 279, Tallahassee, FL 32305-7886 USA
www.dreamspinnerpress.com

What's the Use of Wondering?
© 2017 Kate McMurray.

Cover Art
© 2017 Aaron Anderson.
aaronbydesign55@gmail.com
Cover content is for illustrative purposes only and any person depicted on the cover is a model.

ISBN: 978-1-63533-834-8
Digital ISBN: 978-1-63533-835-5
Library of Congress Control Number: 2017905237
Published July 2017
v. 1.0

Printed in the United States of America

This paper meets the requirements of
ANSI/NISO Z39.48-1992 (Permanence of Paper).

CHAPTER 1

April

THE FIRST time I saw him was on the stage.

This blond Adonis strode out from the wings in a black T-shirt and jeans, with a clipboard in his hand. He was well-muscled perfection, not a hair out of place, and walked with the confidence of a man who commanded the stage. There was a brief moment of serenity when he looked around and smiled, but then he started ordering people around. Or that's how it looked; I couldn't really hear him from where I sat in the orchestra pit, where everyone was tuning.

"Who is *that*?" I asked my best friend and stand partner, Ellie.

She looked up. "That's Peter Bennett. King of the tech crew."

I filed that away for later because our conductor walked over and tapped his baton on a music stand. He held his head high as if he were about to conduct the New York Philharmonic and not the ragtag pit orchestra at a rehearsal for the Western Massachusetts University Theater Club's production of *Guys and Dolls*.

One might have wondered why I, Logan Miller, concertmaster of the WMU orchestra, was sitting in said pit. Apparently this was how I spent my free time. I was a violin major, I was the first sophomore to be named concertmaster in decades, and I chose to play in pit orchestras as an extracurricular activity. In other words, I lived, ate, drank, and breathed violin.

And boys. Whenever I wasn't thinking about bow tension and minor chords, I was thinking about boys.

Hence Peter Bennett, with his perfectly chiseled jaw and his neatly trimmed blond hair and his big shoulders and his thighs—

Lord, he had powerful thighs—snared my attention and continued to distract me throughout rehearsal, even when he was offstage.

He was onstage a lot, though, or at least in the wings. This was the first rehearsal with the orchestra, and he had an unfortunate habit of sticking his head out and making suggestions to tweak what was on the stage.

At first he stuck to telling the tech crew where to put stuff. Most of the sets were painted on wood and set up on wheels so the audience could be quickly transported from the streets of Times Square to the inside of the Save-a-Soul Mission to the underground craps tables where Nathan and the gang gambled. Peter had strong opinions about where exactly things should be onstage, and he'd run out to nudge sets to the left or right, or he'd push props around onstage with his feet until they were positioned within a millimeter of where he thought they should be. His need for control was not limited to tech crew, however; he had a lot to say to the actors as well.

"Hey, Jenny, take three steps forward so your face is more in the light," he yelled at the girl playing Adelaide when she got up to sing a big number. She flinched and did what he said.

As the crew set up the next scene, Peter moved on to another actress. "Kat, you gotta sing louder, honey. No one will be able to hear you from the dead zone in the middle of the theater!"

She rolled her eyes at him.

He seemed particularly obsessed with people not blocking important parts of his sets. When the kid playing Benny Southstreet strolled out with a couple of other cast members to practice the opening number, Peter stuck his head out again. "Chip! Two feet to the right!"

Chuck, the show's actual director, became visibly more annoyed every time Peter did this. He twitched whenever Peter spoke, and spent the entire second half of rehearsal scowling in Peter's direction.

By the time rehearsal wrapped and I was having a postperformance cigarette break at the curb outside the auditorium, I'd pretty much written Peter Bennett off as hot but supremely annoying. I would even have gone as far as to say that his inherent meddling nature made him less hot; I had him pegged as one of those type A control freaks who had to have everything just so, but that's not how theater was, or not how it should be. The beauty of theater was that it was a little rough around the edges, a bit imperfect.

My first cigarette wound down, and I was thinking about having a second before hopping in my car and driving back up the hill to my dorm, when Peter walked out lugging two giant black duffel bags. He dropped the bags near my feet and said, "Hey."

I grunted.

He glanced at the violin case strapped to my back. "String instrument?"

Was he really this dumb? I was willing to buy he hadn't seen me in the pit; he'd been too obsessive about the show's details to have seen beyond the proscenium. And true, it was a rectangular case, not one shaped like a violin, but there weren't many musical instruments that could fit in a case that shape. "Violin," I said.

"Cool. You waiting for a ride?"

"Nope."

That seemed to surprise him; his head bobbed back a little. "So you just hang out on curbs?"

"Sometimes."

"Maggie's bringing the car around." He gestured at the giant bags.

I had no idea who Maggie was, but I pulled out that second cigarette and nodded as I lit it.

"Those will kill you," said Peter.

"Mmm-hmm."

"Just saying."

"I sat through the same health class in high school as you did." I paused to suck on that cancer stick. "Unlike you, I don't spend my Friday nights partying it up in Frat Row and I don't really drink. Let me have my vices."

"He speaks." Peter rolled his eyes. "Okay, first of all, I've never been to a Frat Row party. Well, once, freshman year, but just to see what it was like. Not my scene."

"Point still stands," I said.

"Second of all, I didn't mean anything by my comment. You want to turn your lungs black, be my guest."

I took another pull from my cigarette. "You self-righteous prick. You are, of course, completely without flaws, so you've taken it upon yourself to fix everyone else."

He narrowed his eyes and pointed at me. "You've got it all figured out, don't you?"

I shrugged.

"You don't know jack about me, so maybe cool it with the judgment."

"Who's judging? You're the one who started the antismoking lecture."

"Hardly a lecture. I just pointed out that smoking will kill you. You want to die, that's on you. I don't care what you do." A car pulled up to the curb, and he shouldered one of the bags. "That's Maggie."

I blew a smoke ring at him. He coughed and rolled his eyes again before picking up the other giant duffel.

Perhaps not my finest moment.

"I'm Peter, by the way. Probably we'll be seeing quite a bit of each other over the next few weeks."

Unfortunately. "I'm Logan."

"I'd say it's nice to meet you, but, well, you were here too." He stepped toward the car. A girl I didn't know hopped out and helped him with one of the bags.

"Touché," I said.

I finished off my cigarette as he loaded the trunk and then folded his long body into the passenger seat before the car pulled away. *Asshole.* I put out the butt of my cigarette with the toe of my sneaker. I vowed right there that I'd spend the run of the show avoiding the hell out of Peter Bennett.

CHAPTER 2

September

I'D HAD the same roommate my first two years of college. We weren't friends, exactly, but he was good-natured and friendly, easy to get along with. He was straight but unfazed that I was gay. He was a little bit of a neat freak but didn't mind when I got busy and let my mess accumulate. So I liked having him as a roommate, plus I'd heard so many horror stories about terrible roommate situations that I decided to hang on to him sophomore year. He'd readily agreed.

We were all set to room together junior year, but then he called me in July to inform me he was actually transferring to a school in Boston with a better program for his major, and that left me roommate-less well after the housing change deadline had come and gone. When I called the housing office with the hope I'd just lucked into a single, the woman I talked to said they always had a few kids in my situation, and due to their perpetual housing shortage, they'd find another roommate for me. Unfortunately the form I got in the mail in August had left my roommate's name blank.

Thus I drove into the parking lot behind North Quad four days before the start of the new school year, knowing only that I'd been assigned an unknown roommate. I'd be in the same room in Bishop House that I had been in the previous two years, but with someone else occupying the other bed. I was nervous. I hated the unknown, and given that I was an artsy gay kid who practiced my violin more than I did anything else, there were a lot of variables here. What if my roommate hated music? What if he was loud or messy? What if he was a homophobic asshole?

The last thing I expected when I walked into my room was to see Peter Bennett hanging a poster over the bed on *my* side of the room.

He looked just as handsome as ever, goddamn him.

"Hi!" he said brightly before turning around. "I was wondering when you'd get here, I'm—oh." When he finally recognized me, he frowned. "Ah, the surly smoker. Of course."

I bristled. "Are you… this is…."

"Fraid so." He stepped away from the bed. "Look, this wasn't my first choice either, but my old roommate got a place off campus and Housing gave my room away to a couple of freshmen, so here we are." He glanced up at the poster—it advertised a Rolling Stones concert he wasn't old enough to have attended—and then at me again. "Logan, right?"

"Yeah." I wheeled my suitcases over to the other bed and slid my violin case straps down my shoulders. "I gotta get the rest of my stuff from my car."

"Need a hand?"

I couldn't keep from looking at his arms; he looked strong enough to carry my whole car up the stairs. "No, I got it. I don't have a lot of stuff."

When I came back, he was pulling orange-and-purple striped sheets over the mattress on what was now his bed. I was suddenly thankful for the basement in the Fine Arts Center, where all the music practice rooms were. Being concertmaster gave me certain privileges, including access to a particularly swanky and exclusive practice room pretty much whenever I wanted. I could see myself spending a lot of time there.

"Where did you drive here from?" Peter lifted one of his suitcases to the freshly made bed. I spared a thought for how much dirt was probably caught in the suitcase's wheels that would now be on his clean bedspread, but whatever. If he wanted to live in filth, that was his affair.

Also small talk. Christ. "Springfield. Not far."

He nodded. "I'm from Brookline. My parents just left, like, a half hour ago. This is my third year, so you'd think my mother could leave without turning into a weepy mess, but apparently we're not quite there yet."

My mother had made eggs for breakfast, which was a little unusual, but my parents had otherwise not done anything to commemorate my moving back to school. She might have waved when I got in my car to drive up to campus. I'd been eager to leave. I'd been kind of at loose ends all summer, playing in a community orchestra to give myself something to do and working a few days a week at a men's clothing store in the Holyoke Mall. Most of my high school friends also had jobs and no one's schedules were compatible, so I'd spent a lot of the summer bored out of my skull and hoping for school to start again.

Now I was back on campus and rooming with goddamn Peter Bennett, King of the Tech Crew and Prince of Annoying.

He started unpacking a vast collection of T-shirts, most of them solid-colored but a few advertising sports teams that could have been the fake ones a lot of mall stores put on their novelty tees, for all I knew. There was an actual football wedged into a corner of the suitcase, too, which surprised me for some reason. But, of course, if one were to get involved with theater, tech was the perfect place for an athletic guy who liked throwing things around.

I really had nothing in common with this guy. This year was going to suck out loud.

Still, I decided for my sanity to give him the benefit of the doubt. I opened my own suitcase—on the floor, even though the mattress on my bed was still bare—and started to unpack my clothes, which were mostly fancier fare than jeans and T-shirts. As I hunted around for the bag I'd shoved a bunch of hangers in, I became conscious of Peter watching me.

"You're kind of fussy, aren't you?"

"What makes you say that?" I unfurled a button-down shirt and slid it onto a hanger.

"No wire hangers." He mimed Faye Dunaway as Joan Crawford and then laughed. He pointed to the plastic and fabric-covered hangers now scattered across my bare mattress.

"Cheap hangers put those little points in the shoulders of your shirts. The shirts lie better on the plastic ones."

"See? Fussy."

"Oh, whatever." I wasn't going to justify my sartorial choices to this meathead.

"Hey, dude, do what you want. It just surprised me, given you're a smoker. Which, by the way, I'd prefer you didn't do in the room."

"Not that I could." I gestured toward the smoke detector. "But I mostly quit over the summer." I promised myself I'd only smoke at parties, which had been few and far between, so I'd essentially given it up. I didn't even have a pack on me. I was tempted to take it up again, though, just to annoy him.

"Good," he said.

When I looked up at him, he was grinning. I wanted to tell him to fuck off, but I settled for scowling, which made him grin wider. Then I remembered I meant to give him the benefit of the doubt. "Do you have an issue if I practice my violin in the room? I usually go to the FAC to practice, but sometimes when I'm trying to learn a new piece, I need the extra practice time."

"Yeah, that's fine. As long as it's not, like, the wee hours of the morning."

"No."

Peter pointed at the violin case. "That your major? Music?"

"Yes. And I'm the orchestra concertmaster."

Peter held up his hands. "Oh, well. Of course."

What a jackass. "What's your major?" I wondered if he earned credits for antagonizing roommates.

"Accounting," he said breathily. I couldn't read what his tone meant, but he seemed... displeased. Accounting sounded like a perfectly terrible major, so no wonder. He stepped back toward his bed and put the now-empty suitcase on the floor. "I'm involved in a few campus activities too, so I don't know how much we'll even see each other."

That seemed like good news. I almost asked what activities, but I didn't think I wanted to know. Probably intramural sports. The sort of things I couldn't relate to at all. I bet myself he was one of those guys who ran around the quad playing ultimate Frisbee on nice days. I generally avoided those guys like the plague.

I realized that I was as guilty of stereotyping him as he probably was of me, so I pushed all that aside and went back to unpacking.

"I know this situation isn't ideal," he said, "but for what it's worth, I don't snore and I'm pretty clean."

"Same, although I get kind of scatterbrained right before a concert when we're having rehearsals every day."

"Don't we all?"

I turned around again and he was smiling.

"We'll get along fine," he said.

I doubted this, but I nodded.

CHAPTER 3

ONCE CLASSES started, I barely saw Peter at all, which was just fine with me. He tended to sleep late, so I was usually up and out of the room before he even woke up. He was gone most afternoons, so I studied before evening music classes and rehearsals. If he was back from wherever when I returned from practice, he was either in the room studying or in the lounge down the hall, being social.

It wasn't that I didn't like being social, but I was often so tired after rehearsal that I didn't have much social energy left.

The orchestra director was still settling on what we'd perform at the winter concert in December, so he was putting us through our paces, giving us a lot of challenging music to learn. He seemed to be trying to determine how far he could push us as a collective unit, especially after auditions and six new violins were added.

So when I left orchestra practice one evening in early October and Ellie said, "I feel like my arms are going to fall off," I agreed with the sentiment.

I didn't think about where we were walking, just followed Ellie. She said, "I don't want to rush back. My roommate was being super dramatic this afternoon."

"Again?"

"She's still dating that guy."

"The one who was cheating on her?"

"He's still cheating on her. I saw him making out with some girl at the movie theater last week. But of course, she never believes anyone when they tell her he's sleeping with half the school, because she *loves* him." Ellie rolled her eyes.

"You went to the movies last week? What did you see?"

"Not the point of the story, Logan."

I wasn't terribly invested in Ellie's roommate's drama, except insofar as it stressed Ellie out a good deal of the time. I'd only met Ellie's roommate, Rachel, a couple of times, and she'd seemed fairly nice until she got involved with the drama-causing boyfriend, whose name I couldn't remember.

"Rachel caught him out with another girl this time, so she saw him cheat with her own eyes, and *now* she believes me. Maybe she'll break up with him for good this time, but I doubt it. She still *loves* him. Give me a break."

"I'm sorry she plagues you so much," I said.

"She was all weepy when I left. I didn't know how to help her. A couple of her friends came over, but I just… I can't."

"I get it." I would have avoided the drama too.

Elle paused at a fork in the walkway and looked around. "I'm starving. Did you eat dinner?"

Had I? I couldn't remember, which seemed like a bad sign. "I think I studied through dinner. Music theory test tomorrow."

"Professor Steinway, right? Ugh, that class was brutal. You definitely need to eat, though. Let's go to the Mac."

I hoisted my violin case up on my shoulder and followed Ellie halfway across campus to the Mac, WMU's student center. The building housed a restaurant of the same name that sold burgers, sandwiches, and pastries at all times, so it was still hopping when we got there.

I hadn't realized I was hungry until we were in line for burgers and the scent of grease and sizzling meat hit my nostrils. My stomach gurgled loud enough that Ellie heard it. She slapped me. "Stop forgetting to eat."

"Sorry."

"Don't apologize. Just eat meals regularly."

Once we had our food, we settled in at a table in the middle of everything.

"So how's your semester going?" Ellie asked. "I've hardly seen you except at rehearsal."

"It's fine. More insane than I was expecting. I thought finishing off the last of my general education classes last semester meant the rest of college would be easy because I don't have to take math or science anymore, but these music classes are rough. Plus Costner is kicking my ass." Professor Costner was my violin teacher. He was a good teacher, but he was tough, particularly on me because, as he kept telling me, my potential was so obvious. I was good, but I was concertmaster-of-a-public-university-orchestra good; I hadn't gotten into Juilliard, much to my parents' dismay. I was at WMU on a music scholarship, but that still felt like a consolation prize sometimes.

"Yeah, this semester has been rough so far. I registered for an extra lit class, but I regret that now." Ellie shook her head. "Stay away from Postmodern Lit with Professor Garibaldi."

"So noted."

"Oh, I went to see that new Disney movie. That's why I was at the movies. I went with Gina and Kelsea."

"Did you like the movie?"

"It was really cute! The songs were kind of forgettable, but I liked the story."

Taking two hours out of my day to go to the movies felt like such a luxury, so I hadn't seen a movie in a theater in months. Ellie talked for a minute about what she liked about the movie, and it seemed like it might be worth my time. I wasn't a huge Disney fan, but this one sounded fun.

Ellie munched on some fries and looked around the space. "Hey, isn't that your hot roommate?" She gestured across the room with her head.

I looked. Indeed, there was Peter, seated with a girl I didn't know and a guy I recognized vaguely.

"That's Dave... something," Ellie said. "He was in my lit class last semester. I think he lives in Emerson, maybe?"

I recognized this Dave as one of the ultimate Frisbee guys. "Right, okay. I don't know the girl."

"No, me neither."

We watched them for a moment. The girl had long brown hair and was wearing a navy blue dress with big white polka dots. She kept playfully punching Peter, which I supposed was probably flirting. "Think that's his girlfriend?" I asked.

"Beats me. Oh, did you hear the Theater Club is doing *Oklahoma!* this semester? Are you going to do pit orchestra again?"

I couldn't tear my gaze away from Peter, though I knew I was staring like a crazy person. I tried to focus on Ellie and her questions. "I don't think I can do pit. Costner has me doing one extra class every week, and I think it's the same time as pit orchestra rehearsal."

"It's not that rehearsal has a time, per se, so much as just meets whenever everyone is available."

I shook my head. "I want to, but I don't have enough spare time this semester. Sorry."

"Bummer. It won't be the same without you."

We ate silently for a moment. I kept watching Peter out of the corner of my eye. The girl was basically hanging on him, but she did the flirty punch thing with Dave too. I couldn't really figure out what the deal was, but Peter was probably friends with the jock types, and they all probably lifted weights and grunted and did... masculine... things together. I didn't know what non-music majors got up to in their free time. It was all probably super homoerotic even though they were all straight guys—or it was in my overactive, sleep-deprived imagination—and then I was down some rabbit hole, picturing Dave and Peter making out with each other in a pile of other men, everyone writhing together.

"Ugh," I said.

"If you're not even eating regularly, I guess you're not dating either."

I looked back at Ellie, who was always an unrepentant gossip. "Who would I date? I only see orchestra people. Who am I supposed to go out with? Richard?"

We both laughed at that. Richard was a skinny little twerp viola player who was a gifted musician but a real pill in person.

Everyone had been telling him for years how wonderful he was, and he believed them wholeheartedly.

Ellie shook her head. "This is not what college is for, you know. You should be meeting people, going to parties, having fun. And by fun, I mean sex."

"Tell that to my parents."

Ellie sighed. "I know."

I watched Peter horse around with Dave and the girl, a little bit curious about his personal life but not enough to do something foolish like actually ask him about it. Instead I turned my attention back to my dinner and let Ellie talk my ear off about who *was* dating each other in the orchestra. The gossip distracted me from my handsome roommate, but barely.

I CAME home from rehearsal a few nights later and found Peter and the long-haired girl sitting together on his bed. It wasn't like I walked in on them doing anything scandalous; they sat side by side while watching something on Peter's tiny TV and giggling a lot, but Peter did have his arm thrown around her.

"Hi." I put my violin case away in its spot at the foot of my bed.

"Oh, hey, Logan." Peter shuffled forward a little, removing his arm from around the girl. "This is Lily."

"Hi. I'm Logan."

"I gathered," Lily said with a wry smile. She held out her hand to be shaken, so I shook it.

"Fall TV is back," Peter said. "Lily and I always watch *Piper Hill* together."

I had never been much for TV—my parents banned it for most of my childhood—but I lived in the world, so I knew *Piper Hill* was a nighttime soap. "I've never seen it," I said.

"Seriously?" said Lily.

"I don't really watch TV."

"What kind of American are you?"

Peter clapped a hand on his mouth, clearly suppressing a laugh. "Watch with us, then," he said. "I guarantee it will suck you in."

For once I didn't have to study, so I sat on my own bed and toed off my shoes. By the time I'd settled my back against my pillows, the commercial break had ended. I watched for a few minutes as a blonde woman had a rather passionate argument with a brown-haired man. I had no idea what the argument was about or why I was watching this, but by the time the next commercial break rolled around, I was hooked.

"What's the deal with Rebecca?" I asked.

Peter and Lily took turns explaining the backstory on the characters who had just been gracing our screen. They were so enthusiastic about the show, they reminded me of Professor Costner talking about Mendelssohn. I had a pretty good handle on the particulars of some of the characters when the show came back, but these scenes involved different characters, and I was lost again. And so it went until the end of the episode, when I had a shaky grasp on what was going on in the show, but still had trouble keeping all the characters' names straight.

Peter and Lily had no such problem.

"I can't get over Naomi," Lily said when Peter put the TV on mute so they could talk. "She's clearly in love with Noah, but she's still going out with Ted."

"I still ship Noah and Naomi so hard," said Peter. "I don't know why the show keeps breaking them up. They clearly belong together."

Lily laughed. "Totally. Then that whole thing with Rebecca and Drake."

Peter rolled his eyes. "Ugh, don't get me started. Drake is a tool."

"He is not! God, he's dreamy. You don't think so?"

Peter scoffed. "You clearly have no taste. His face is so weird. Like his eyes are too close together or something."

"Him looking weird doesn't make him a tool."

"No, his jerking around Rebecca makes him a tool. Do you think he killed Erica?"

"No. I bet it was Rebecca."

"Girl, you are crazy." They both laughed.

It was a strange thing to watch. I figured this was the way couples often operated, but I wouldn't have known. I'd dated a little in my time at WMU, and I was hardly a virgin, but violin so dominated my life that I hadn't ever really had a relationship.

I was missing out.

I was intensely jealous of the rapport Peter had with Lily, of the easy way they related to each other. I had friends, sure, but not a romantic relationship, and as I watched Peter walk Lily to the door and give her a quick peck on the cheek, I yearned for one.

Until that moment, I hadn't appreciated how lonely I was.

I rested my head on the wall behind my low wooden headboard and sighed as Peter came back into the room and softly closed the door.

"You okay?" he asked.

"Yeah." I was hardly going to get into my stupid little personal crisis with stupid hot Peter.

Today his blond hair was a little disheveled, and he was wearing a blue T-shirt with a big green T. rex on the front, stretched over his substantial pectoral muscles. His jeans were a little baggy, but not so much that they didn't nicely highlight those thighs, and I might have stared a little as he sat back down on his bed and mimicked my pose.

"I'll convert you to a soap fan by the end of the semester," he said.

"Huh?"

He grinned. "I know it's totally ridiculous, but I love this kind of garbage TV. Everyone has worse problems than I do, you know?"

I seriously doubted Peter had any problems. He was gorgeous, he never seemed stressed, and he had the sort of major that led to financial stability. Because he'd probably finish college and get a job right away, whereas I'd leave WMU with a bachelor of fine arts in violin performance—with minor debt because of the scholarship, granted—but no guarantee of anything except a lifetime of auditions.

I stifled another sigh. I didn't want to seem like too much of a sad sack. So I said, "It was entertaining."

Peter chuckled. "Oh, sure. Say it all proper like that. 'It was entertaining.' Don't you ever have fun?"

Probably not. "Playing in pit orchestra is fun." It was, actually, now that I thought about it. There was less expectation in pit orchestra, less perfection required. It was recreational, not for the sake of impressing anyone. Most of the people who played in pit weren't music majors; instead ensembles across campus were populated by kids who'd played in their high school bands and orchestras and hadn't given up their instruments, but weren't interested in majoring in music. They just wanted to play. No one was telling the pit orchestra that this semester's production of *Oklahoma!* Was their ticket into the Boston Pops or the New York Philharmonic, like Costner kept saying about the December concert.

"Oh, are you going to do pit orchestra again? Because I'm doing tech on *Oklahoma!* And the guy playing Curly is really good. I saw him sing the other day."

"You really like doing tech."

He shrugged. "I like musicals. I can't really act or sing, so this is my contribution to the Theater Club."

It was a good answer, but something about it seemed inaccurate or inauthentic to me. I supposed it made more sense than Peter just having a general desire to lift heavy things. "Okay," I said. "I'm not sure about pit orchestra. It's looking like it won't work with my schedule this semester."

"That sucks. Maybe next semester, then. A bunch of the kids in the club want to do *Hair* or *Rent*, but we'll probably end up doing something safe and vanilla like *Bye Bye Birdie* or *Sweet Charity*. There'd still be a pit orchestra, though, obviously." He smirked. "I've heard you play, and you don't suck."

"Yeah, maybe," I said, returning his crooked smile. "I've heard rumors. We'll see about next semester."

The conversation died after that. Peter picked up his remote and started flipping through channels, so I got up and grabbed my music theory book and my laptop to do my homework.

"Some of the guys from the Theater Club are having a party Saturday night," Peter said just as I powered on my laptop. "You should come. I think it would do you good to not study or practice for five minutes."

I didn't like him deciding what would be good or not for me, but I didn't hate the idea of a party. "I'll think about it."

"I'll drag you if I have to."

I bristled, an instinctive reaction to him bossing me around, but I quickly reasoned that Ellie was probably going, if it was a Theater Club do. "That won't be necessary. I'll go."

He smiled and nodded. "Good."

As I got into working on my assignment, though, I kept wondering why Peter cared so much. It was nice of him to invite me, but why was he being so insistent? Was I really that much of a wet blanket that people felt they needed to force me to lighten up for my own good?

I wanted to groan when I realized that yes, probably this was true. But I kept that thought to myself.

CHAPTER 4

COSTNER STOOD off to the side as I played a run of sixteenth notes. The whole thing was about ten bars, but every time I got to the end of it and started to move on to the next section of the piece, Costner yelled at me to start over at the beginning of the phrase. The first three times I'd played through it, I'd corrected something I'd been doing wrong. I'd misread the key signature and kept playing the D-flat too sharp, so I fixed that but then realized I was playing a couple of eighth notes in the middle of the run as sixteenth notes, so I fixed *that*, but then Costner didn't like the pace. By the time I was playing it perfectly, Costner made me repeat it three times just to make sure I could do it. I did, but I found his hovering unnerving.

"You know that I give you a hard time because I know you're good enough," Costner said as I packed up. "You have the discipline to handle the extra rehearsals this year. The solo at the December concert is going to blow everyone out of the water."

"Thanks," I said, zipping up my case.

"I'm inviting a number of conductors and directors to the concert. Any of them would be lucky to have you in their orchestra."

I paused what I was doing to let that sink in. Was he implying I should leave school? "I still have at least three semesters of school left."

Costner waved his hand as if this were immaterial. "I happen to know there will be an opening in the Boston Symphony at the end of the year. You're a brilliant musician, and if you keep playing like this, that spot is yours."

My stomach flopped. "And not finish school?"

"Believe me, Logan, I want to keep working with you, but not if the college orchestra is holding you back. If you made the Boston

Symphony at your age, you'd be set for life. And now is the time to take that opportunity, because spots don't open up very often."

A wave of nausea hit me. Why was everyone so determined to push me into the real world so fast? Wasn't college supposed to be the time one went to parties and met people and hooked up and had fun? Was I really spending my junior year stuck at extra rehearsals, feeling exhausted all the time, never seeing other people?

"I'll think about it," I said, although I couldn't decide whether I was trying to convince myself or Costner that I was okay with this. Was I ready to play in a big orchestra? Was that what I even wanted? My heart pounded as I closed my violin case.

"In the meantime, I'd like to set up extra violin rehearsals for the orchestra. I think the first violins need extra practice to get the Bach piece right in time for the concert. Maybe Tuesdays? Could you lead a rehearsal then?"

There went my last free night of the week. My heart sank. "Sure."

"Great! I'll see if I can get the rehearsal space and send an e-mail."

I trudged back up to my dorm room feeling overwhelmed. I mentally reviewed my weekly evening schedule: orchestra rehearsals on Mondays and Wednesdays, one-on-one class with Costner on Thursday, and now this extra sectional on Tuesdays, and that was my whole week. It felt daunting. All violin all the time. Oh, and an orchestra somewhere else in the country might want me to play for them.

I walked past the lounge on my floor and spotted Peter and a couple of the guys from down the hall playing some violent video game. That was what I was supposed to be doing as a college student: goofing off on a Thursday night. Hell, Ellie didn't even have Friday classes, so she always joked that her weekend started Thursday night. If only.

I sighed as I crossed the threshold into my room and put my violin away. I texted Ellie to tell her about the extra rehearsal, and she responded within a moment: *Costner just ate your whole schedule.*

Yup, I said.

I flopped face-first on the bed.

"You okay?" Peter asked. Apparently he'd walked into the room while I was being dramatic.

I rolled onto my back. "Yeah. Just some stupid orchestra scheduling nonsense. Not a big deal, just annoying."

"Okay."

"I'm tired. Sorry."

"Want me to leave?"

"No, it's fine."

I looked up at him. He stood in the middle of the room, his brow furrowed in concern. Why he cared, I had no idea. But there he was, wearing skinny jeans that strained against his thighs, and a black T-shirt. His hair looked soft, like he'd washed it recently, and I briefly entertained a fantasy in which he'd let me run my fingers through it. He continued to peer at me as though he expected me to say something.

So I said, "Junior year was supposed to be fun, but instead I just go to rehearsal all the time. I feel like I should be, I don't know, meeting more people or going to parties or something, but it's all violin all the time."

"That blows."

I sat up. "It's not great. Not to unload on you. I didn't mean to pull you away from your video games."

"It's fine. We were done. I have homework due tomorrow anyway. Just blowing off steam before I have to spend an hour solving math problems." He grimaced.

"Sounds fun."

"I'd rather blow stuff up. Luke got this new game…."

And then Peter was off to the races. I didn't know who Luke was and I'd never heard of the game franchise Peter was talking about, even though he'd apparently been playing its third iteration. So I mostly listened while he rattled on and took a heavy-looking textbook off his bookshelf.

I'm pretty sure he was still talking when I fell asleep.

I woke up a little while later and spotted him across the room at his desk, wearing only a thin white tank top and threadbare sleep pants. My first thought was that there was a very thin barrier between his hot naked body and the air. Then I groaned, because he was straight and I'd fallen asleep while he was trying to tell me something, hadn't I?

He turned around. "Oh, hey, sleepyhead."

I sat up. "Sorry I fell asleep on you. Guess I was tired."

He smiled. "It's fine. It wasn't important. I was just rambling. I don't even know what I was talking about."

I rubbed my forehead and tried to take an assessment of what was going on around me. My backpack sat on the foot of the bed, reminding me I had a homework assignment due the next day. I swung my feet onto the floor and fished in my pocket, hoping I had enough change for the vending machine in the lounge. I stood and moved toward the door. "I'm going to go get a Coke. I need some caffeine if I'm going to finish this assignment. You want something?"

"No need!" Peter reached for the minifridge near his desk and pulled out a can of soda. Then he stood and walked over to me. "I bought a case. Consider it communal."

"Are you sure?"

"Yeah. It's no problem."

I must have been really out of it, because I said, "That's so nice," as if he'd just brought me flowers and chocolates instead of a can of soda that had a small dent in it.

"Seriously, the whole case cost, like, three bucks at the store in the Mac. It's no big deal."

He passed me the can, and our fingers brushed as I took it. His hands were bigger than mine. He had bulky workman's hands, wide palms with meaty fingers, and I had long, delicate violin-player fingers. His skin had some color, a light tan that was likely from running around the quad playing touch football, but I was pale as a sheet. The contrast was striking. And electric. At the brush of his fingers, I looked up and met his gaze. I got stuck there for a moment while he stared back at me.

Then he smiled sideways and winked. "You can get the next case."

"Case?"

"Of sodas. Might as well share."

"Right. Of course."

He sat back at his desk and returned to his work. I felt out of sorts now, though. My attraction to my roommate was a big problem. And I knew he wasn't making overtures or anything; he probably just wanted to keep the peace between us to make this year as pleasant as possible, and I wasn't helping matters by being so irritable.

I let out a breath and sat on my bed. Peter Bennett probably wasn't a bad guy. A little annoying and sexy as hell, but maybe not the worst roommate I could have had. So decided, I cracked open the can and got out my homework.

CHAPTER 5

THE THEATER Club party was in a basement room at the Mac. I followed Peter into the room and took in the decorations. Leave it to theater kids to go a little over the top with their artistic achievements when decorating for a party. The whole room was like a theater dork's wet dream. It was a tribute to Rodgers & Hammerstein, with walls covered in posters for actual productions of *Oklahoma!* and *Carousel* and *The Sound of Music* as well as handmade signs with song lyrics and photos of Julie Andrews and Hugh Jackman and the like framed with colorful mattes. The actors in that year's production all had name tags with their characters' names. It was supremely nerdy. Peter's whole face lit up when he saw it.

"It looks amazing, doesn't it? How great is this?"

"It's nice," I said.

Ellie was already there, flirting shamelessly with a guy who had a name tag that read *Curly*. She saw me, gave me a little wave, and then went back to flirting. I was already uncomfortable enough that I turned toward the door, ready to march out of there, but Peter caught my arm. "Oh, no, you don't."

"Is there any booze at this shindig?" I asked.

Peter shrugged. "This is an official university function. Could you get in trouble with the administration for drinking booze?"

I was only twenty, so I said, "Fair point." I grunted. "Unfortunately we can't all have your social ease. Some of us need a little lubrication."

If he noticed my accidental double entendre, he didn't acknowledge it. As a flush overcame me, he rolled his eyes. "Is coming to a party really wigging you out that much?"

I took a deep breath. "I guess not."

Music suddenly filled the room. I didn't recognize the tune at first, but by the way the key and the melody kept changing, I understood it was the overture to a musical. Of course. I didn't understand someone had put on the soundtrack to *Oklahoma!* until the entire room burst into a flat, loud rendition of "Oh, What a Beautiful Mornin'."

I felt myself shutting down. I didn't know what was wrong with me, but in the face of this much unbridled joy, I turned in on myself. It wasn't that I didn't like musicals; I did, or I wouldn't have done pit orchestra so many times. It wasn't even that I disliked the Theater Club kids, because I'd been to functions like this before and had a fine time. But something about this particular confluence of circumstances—Peter, the difficult semester, me not knowing half the kids in the room—made me feel suddenly, starkly alone.

"Do you think there's something to eat at least?" I asked Peter over the din of his friends singing. I felt okay asking because he was not singing, though he was clearly hanging on every word.

He just pointed to a refreshment table in the corner.

This particular song was apparently a popular one, because the singing did not continue when the tracks changed. Well, a few kids kept singing, but the party quieted down and everyone started chatting instead. There was a blond guy standing at the refreshment table, lingering over a plate of minicupcakes. When I approached, I saw it was Noel, one of the Theater Club regulars and another junior. Noel and I had run into each other at rehearsals all the time, so we were friendly but not very close. He wore a name tag now that said *Will Parker*.

"Hi," I said.

"Oh, hey, Logan." He smiled at me. "To cupcake or not to cupcake."

"It's a party. Go for it."

He snatched one. "Nice to see you. Are you doing pit orchestra this semester?"

"No, unfortunately. I'm too busy with orchestra rehearsals. I'm crashing your party. Well, I came with my roommate. Peter Bennett?"

"King of the Tech Crew Peter Bennett? Yeah, he mentioned he had a new roommate who was kind of a sourpuss. I should have put that together."

"Hey!" I pretended to be offended, but I couldn't argue with that characterization of me, given how that semester had been going.

Noel grinned. "Well, as an outsider, what do you think of our little fete?"

"It's nice. You guys outdid yourselves with the decorations."

"I know, right? I helped, but actually, my boyfriend came up with a lot of the ideas for this. He's the biggest theater queen I've ever met with zero musical talent. Like, he loves musicals, but no one should ever let him sing. I love him anyway." A brief bit of sadness fell over Noel's beautiful face. "Unfortunately he had to work tonight and couldn't find anyone to trade shifts with. He would have loved this, though."

"That sucks."

Noel shrugged. "Well, anyway. How are you? Haven't seen you in a while."

"I'm… busy."

"Right. With orchestra rehearsals?"

"Yeah. We're doing a really challenging program for the December concert, so I'm doing extra rehearsals and classes."

I paused to look around the room and then glanced down at the refreshment table. In addition to the minicupcakes, there were cookies that looked homemade, a bowl full of chips, another full of pretzels, and a few two-liter bottles of soda and lemonade. I grabbed a cup and poured myself some lemonade.

"The Queer Student Union is doing an LGBT semiformal again this year," Noel said. "You should come."

I found the Queer Student Union generally exhausting, so I shrugged. "Sure, I guess. If I'm free."

"I know you haven't been to a meeting in forever, but it's a good group this year. The new president is really nice."

"I'm sure. Are the cupcakes any good?"

He peeled the wrapper off the bottom and popped the whole thing in his mouth. As he chewed, he gave me the thumbs-up.

I laughed despite myself. Noel was one of the most beautiful people at WMU—kind of androgynous with white-blond hair and startling blue eyes—and seeing him with cheeks stuffed with cupcake was so absurd I couldn't keep the giggles at bay. He grinned after he swallowed.

"I suppose if I came to this dance, I'd have to bring a date," I said.

"You don't have to. It's mostly just an excuse to look fancy and dance in a big mob. I'll bring my boyfriend, of course, but he's on the planning committee anyway."

I was a little sad I didn't have the opportunity to meet this enterprising young man. Given the flush that spread across Noel's cheeks, he was quite smitten. Anyone as good-looking as Noel couldn't have possibly stayed single for long. WMU didn't have a huge LGBT population, but there were enough of us around that there was a decent-sized dating pool. I was glad Noel had found happiness, but I had that pang of jealousy again that I'd experienced when I'd watched Peter and Lily. It wasn't that I wanted Noel, who wasn't really my type anyway; I wanted what Noel had, I wanted to feel whatever he did when he thought about his boyfriend.

How the hell was I supposed to find it? It wasn't like I had time to look.

But I should have. Ellie was right: the point of college wasn't to kill yourself working, but to meet people. Maybe I should have been putting more effort into meeting people.

"When does the QSU meet again?" I asked.

"Tuesday afternoons. The info is on the website."

"Okay. Maybe I'll pop in to a meeting." Although as soon as I said it, I remembered the new violin sectional. Dammit.

"Great!"

Noel opened his mouth to speak again, but someone across the room shouted, "Hey, Will Parker, get your ass over here."

Noel hooked his thumb back toward his summoner. "I better go. Have fun at the party!"

I watched him walk away and then turned my attention toward gathering snack food. I put a cupcake, a cookie, and some chips on a little paper plate decorated with cowboys and lassos. Ellie wandered over as I was shoving the cookie in my mouth.

"This is not completely terrible," she said. "I saw you flirting with Noel."

"We weren't flirting. Just chatting. He has a boyfriend he couldn't stop talking about." I ate a couple of chips.

"Oh. I thought he and Jason broke up."

"Could be a different guy. I don't think he said his boyfriend's name."

Ellie looked around. "Well, this is a Theater Club party. There have to be some single gay guys here besides you."

I tried to work out how to get the wrapper off my cupcake while still holding the plate. I nodded to concede she was probably right. I had to put the plate down to get the wrapper off, but once I accomplished that, I said, "Are you trying to matchmake me?"

"Maybe." She grabbed a cookie and popped it in her mouth.

She was attempting to help me, but I felt like an astronaut floating outside the space station, not an active participant in this party. "Am I totally lame?"

"What? No. Why do you ask that?"

"I'm single. I don't go out... ever, really. I don't have very many friends, present company aside."

"You're training to be a concert violinist. That takes a lot of work."

"Yeah, but... what if I don't want to be a concert violinist?"

It was the first time I'd ever said that out loud, but definitely not the first time I'd thought it. My parents had been paying for lessons since I was three years old, with the hopes of raising the next Joshua Bell, but I was no prodigy, and you couldn't force that into a kid. I was good by virtue of the fact that I spent so many hours practicing, and I'd been made concertmaster in part because of my insane work ethic, but what if the rest of my life suffered because of those hours I put in? What if I never met the right man, got married, had a family? Or, hell, what if I never had fun? Somehow I'd forgotten how.

"What do you mean, what if you don't want to?" Ellie stared at me like I'd just grown an arm out of my forehead.

"I mean, maybe being a performance major is eating too much of my time. I should spend more time, I don't know, going to parties and meeting hot guys."

She looked aghast. "Are you feeling okay?"

"Just thinking aloud. You were right. Costner is eating my whole semester."

"So don't let him."

"Easy for you to say. You're not a performance major," I pointed out. Ellie was majoring in music education. "I can't just tell Costner I'm not coming to rehearsal. And I… you don't get how hard it is."

She flinched. "Maybe not, but I'm not good enough to do more than sit in the back of the orchestra."

"That's not true. If you worked—" I held up my hand. "No, I'm going to stop myself. I think you've got the right of it. You have time to breathe."

"And eat regularly."

I had a second cupcake halfway to my mouth. I *was* starving, probably because I'd forgotten to eat lunch again. After I ate the cupcake, I said, "If I switched majors to music ed, do you think I'd have more free time?"

"Probably, but first of all, Costner would kill you, as would your parents, and second, you'd have to take another year of classes."

All of that was true. "Forget it. It was a dumb idea."

Ellie frowned. She grabbed a handful of chips and munched on them for a moment. "I'm not saying don't do it if it's what you want, but make sure it's what you want before you change majors. I mean, you're probably going to get offers from major orchestras when you graduate. Everyone knows how talented you are. Do you really want to throw that away?"

"I guess not." But I kind of did. Being in a major orchestra was my parents' dream for me. I had only ever wanted to play, but not at the exclusion of all other things in my life. Maybe it was foolish to hope for anything else. Ellie was right, I'd be squandering a great opportunity, but if I were a music teacher instead of a musician, I could do so many other things. I could play for fun and teach kids to play. I could direct a high school orchestra. That seemed like something I'd be good at. Every time I thought about playing with a big professional orchestra, I wanted to vomit. Which was probably all the information I needed that I was on the wrong track. "Just a thought," I said.

Ellie ate some more chips. "*Are* you okay?"

I wasn't. I was so lonely, it still felt like I was a world apart from these kids. "I'm fine."

Peter wandered over. He surveyed the snack offerings and took a single pretzel from the bowl. "Having fun?"

"Your friends are dorks, but yes."

He winked. Then he turned the full force of his considerable charm on Ellie. "Hi, I'm Peter. Logan's roommate."

"Yeah," Ellie said. "I played in the pit orchestra for *Guys and Dolls*. We met last year? I'm in the pit for *Oklahoma!* too."

He narrowed his eyes, but then realization dawned and he pointed at her. "Oh, yeah! I remember you now. Ellie, right?"

"Yup." She smiled.

Great. I could see the whole rest of the semester playing out before me. Peter would be utterly charmed by Ellie, as well he should, because she was great. He'd dump long-haired Lily and ask out Ellie, and then they'd wander off into the sunset and have a bunch of babies and I'd have to kill them both.

I really was a miserable bastard.

I considered asking Peter why he'd brought me to this party instead of Lily, but I wasn't even really sure she was his girlfriend and not a good friend, and maybe she hated the Theater Club kids, and I just didn't know how to ask the question. Instead, I tossed my little cowboy plate into the trash and rocked on my heels.

Someone changed the music. Still Rodgers & Hammerstein, but music I didn't recognize. "Which show is this from?" I asked.

Ellie and Peter both listened for a few bars. "*Carousel*, I think," said Ellie.

"Oh, yeah." Peter grimaced comically. "I never liked this show as much."

He was apparently in the minority, because a bunch of the girls on one side of the room took the opportunity to sing along with the soundtrack. I recognized a few of the songs from my high school orchestra days—my high school orchestra director had been a big fan of musicals, especially Andrew Lloyd Webber, but Rodgers & Hammerstein too—but Peter was right, this show wasn't as good as *Oklahoma!*

And, because this was the Theater Club and Ellie was right about me not being the only gay guy at this party, everyone singing along seemed to particularly relish singing, "You're a *queer* one, Julie Jordan!" Two of the girls even kissed.

"I don't think that's what the lyrics mean," I said.

Ellie elbowed me. "You're no fun at all."

I spent the next portion of the party doing my best wallflower imitation, hanging around the refreshment table and feebly making small talk with whoever came by to eat chips. Ellie did a far better job of mingling, and at one point brought over a cute guy named Craig whose name tag said *Jud*. The implication was clear, though Craig seemed oblivious to Ellie's machinations. She left us alone for a few minutes, during which time Craig said, "You remind me of my ex," in a way that indicated this was not a good thing, and that was that.

The impromptu production of *Carousel* got progressively gayer as the night wore on. They gender-swapped a bunch of the characters, with girls taking male roles and guys taking female roles and characters swapping songs. They even got Peter involved, and no, he didn't have a great singing voice, but it was passable. He butchered "What's the Use of Wond'rin'," mostly because he didn't seem to know the lyrics aside from the main chorus bit about how someone had a feller and she loved him. One of the girls sang over him and seemed to be singing the song *to* Peter, gesturing to one of the other guys in the crowd, which made Peter blush and wave his hands as if this were absurd and the very notion made him uncomfortable.

Then again, this was... fun. Even if I wasn't directly participating, I liked the queer spin the Theater Club kids were putting on the show tunes, which made the whole room feel like a safe place to be gay. I wanted to shed my stupid hang-ups and social anxiety and throw myself into this party with gusto, to be myself, except I wasn't entirely sure who I was apart from my violin.

I made a promise to myself then. I would find out who I really was that semester, before it was too late to change the course of my life.

CHAPTER 6

I WAS in my room studying when Peter breezed in one afternoon, wearing his gym clothes, muttering about needing to change before he had to get to the auditorium for Theater Club. He dumped his backpack on the bed and then moved to the dresser, where he pulled out a black T-shirt and a clean pair of jeans. I watched the back view—I was only human, and Peter had a great ass—and before I could feel guilty for ogling my straight roommate, he turned around and grabbed the front of his shirt and tugged on it a couple of times.

"Lord, I smell ripe. I better shower before I go out again." He whipped the offending shirt right over his head. And… there were his abs.

I still didn't know what to do with Peter half the time. Lily was in my room often enough that I assumed they were dating, but I never caught them doing anything more than snuggling on Peter's bed when they watched TV. And thank goodness for that; my eyeballs might have caught fire if I'd walked in on them in flagrante. I had caught him playing touch football with the North Quad football brigade, as I'd dubbed the guys who ran around the field behind Emerson House, playing sports on warm afternoons. Not to stereotype, but this seemed to point to his being heterosexual. Yet he hung out with the Theater Club kids, and they all seemed to like him more than I did, so it was possible I'd misjudged him. On the other, other hand, he was very careful about changing clothes in front of me, ducking into the little alcove in one corner of the room so that I never saw him naked. I'd afforded him the same courtesy. My previous roommate had done that too, but he'd been quite vocal about not wanting any nudity in the room.

I hadn't come out to Peter, but I assumed he knew. I tended to ping people's gaydar, and we knew so many people in common that someone had probably mentioned what my deal was.

Or did he not know?

Well, whatever the situation was, he stood in front of me, now shirtless, and it was a sight to behold. Being this attracted to my straight roommate was a problem, even if he was A-OK with the LGBT set.

He toed off his sneakers and socks, slid his feet into flip-flops, grabbed his shower caddy and towel, and walked out of the room.

I was crazy turned on.

I tried to go back to my musical arrangement homework, hoping the problem of how to fix the section I was stuck on would be enough of a boner killer that I wouldn't embarrass myself when Peter got back. That didn't really work; I was incredibly distracted by the knowledge that he was showering, even if it was all the way down the hall. I couldn't keep myself from picturing him standing in that gray stall, water sluicing down his naked, muscular body, over his shoulders, his pecs, his abs, his cock. I stared at the page of musical notes in front of me, trying to focus on the lines and ovals instead of Peter's hypothetical naked body.

Dammit.

He came back wearing only a towel, and he had to walk past me to get to the clothes he'd left on his bed, so now he was *in the room* nearly naked and also *wet*, and I almost died.

He ducked into the alcove and pulled the cheap curtain we'd put up for privacy. While he changed, he said conversationally, "We're painting sets today."

What this had to do with me, I knew not, but I said, "Okay."

He emerged from the alcove, dressed but with the towel still in his hand. He used it to rub his hair before hanging it on the hook behind our door. His hair stuck out every which way. "It's my favorite part of tech," he said.

"Oh. Good. Have fun."

He gave me a strange look, and I understood suddenly that he was trying to engage me in conversation.

"Sorry," I said. "I didn't mean that to sound so sarcastic. That's cool about painting the sets. Are you building a big farm or what?"

He whipped out a comb from somewhere and ran it through his hair. "Yeah, kind of. I mean, I've never been to Oklahoma, but there's, like, corn and stuff, right?"

I laughed. "Yes, probably. I've never been either."

He chuckled and tossed the comb at his desk. Then his phone beeped and he grabbed it. "Ugh, what the hell?"

"What is it?"

He frowned. "Made the mistake of giving my phone number to the wrong person, and he keeps texting me to ask me out. Not happening, dude." He stabbed the screen with his thumb a few times.

Taken aback a bit, I watched his fingers fly over his phone screen. Thinking about Peter in the context of another guy hitting on him was wacky; I'd only ever really seen him with Lily. I wished I could slip into Peter's head and work out what he was thinking. "Did you know he was going to ask you out when you gave him your number?"

"No. He said he wanted to help with the set design for *Oklahoma!*, but apparently he really just wants to get into my pants. I hate when this happens."

I couldn't tell if he was mad at this guy in particular or guys asking him out generally. I thought about what to say. "That happens a lot? Guys asking you out?"

He stared at me blankly for a moment. He hesitated, probably also thinking through what to say. "Yeah, I guess. Guys. Girls. I just… I think I'm too trusting, you know? I mean, if someone came to you and was like, 'Hey, I'd like to learn violin,' and you set up classes or whatever, but really it was a pretense to come on to you, you'd be kind of pissed, right?"

"Depends on how hot this person was," I said, trying for a joke.

"Ha. Well, this guy is not all that. And, like, I guess I don't mind that he tried to get to know me through Theater Club, because that's cool and all, but after I told him I was flattered but not interested, he won't back off."

Ugh. *Flattered* was straight-guy language for *I ain't gay, but I'm trying not to seem offended you came on to me.* "That sucks," I said for lack of anything better to say.

"Yeah. Anyway. I'm late. I better run. I'll see you later, Logan."

He headed out the door.

A COUPLE of hours later, after that night's rehearsal, I was back in my room studying when my parents called.

My mother had grown up in the Dorchester neighborhood of Boston and had a pretty pronounced accent, though she'd trained her whole life to get rid of it. It meant that when she was trying to sound smart or impressive, she overcorrected and pronounced R-controlled syllables with extra emphasis.

She said, "Darling, I just got off the phone with Roger Paxton. He's a violinist with the Boston Pops."

"Okay," I said.

"That's your dream orchestra, isn't it? He's willing to work with you when you're home during the holidays. Kind of like a mentor. He's been playing with them for three years, so he can give you the inside scoop, introduce you to the right people. He's from right here in Springfield. His mother is in my yoga class. Isn't that wild?"

"That's great, Mom. Thanks."

"I knew you'd be happy." She clearly hadn't read my tone. "It's very important to take every opportunity you're given. Speaking of, what are you doing right now? Isn't this a rehearsal night?"

"It is, yeah, but rehearsal ended an hour ago. I'm studying."

"Yes. Very important to keep up your studies. Best possible résumé, you know? Since you didn't get into Juilliard or Berklee."

I sighed. "Yeah."

My father picked up the extension. "Listen to your mother, son. Maybe this Roger fellow will do some extra practice with you."

Right. Because if there was one thing my life lacked, it was opportunities to practice my violin. "Thanks, guys. I appreciate the opportunity."

"You don't sound like you do," said Dad. "This guy could be your ticket into the orchestra."

"We just want what's best for you, Logan," said Mom. "We'd be so proud of you if you made it into an orchestra like the Boston Pops. It's what you've been working toward for so long."

That nauseous feeling I got when Professor Costner started talking about orchestra scouts coming to the December concert came back. Roger Paxton was probably a perfectly nice guy, but I was starting to resent everyone planning my future for me without consulting me. There had been a time when I would have walked over both of my parents to be in the Boston Pops, when I'd felt a pang whenever I listened to one of their recordings and pictured myself sitting among them, but that time had passed. Instead I wanted to go hide in a cabin somewhere where nobody cared if I played music or not, where I wasn't letting anyone down if I took a goddamned night off.

"I do appreciate the opportunity. Give me Mr. Paxton's contact info and I'll reach out to him. Okay?"

About three minutes after I hung up with my parents, I got a text from Ellie that read *Peter fell off a ladder. Going to ER.*

It shocked me so much I almost fell out of my chair. My angst about orchestras and my parents was instantly forgotten. If Peter was hurt bad enough to go to the ER, was it serious? Did he hit his head? Break his spine? Was his life in danger?

Rather than asking a rational question, I texted back, *What?!?!*

It took her a moment, but then she wrote back, *Maybe broken leg?*

So it probably wasn't a life-threatening injury. *Did someone go with him to the hospital?*

Maggie is what she texted back.

Who the hell was Maggie?

I realized, as I was in the process of texting this question, that Maggie was Peter's friend from the tech crew, the one who had a car. I thought about working out how to get in touch with Peter to offer him a ride home, but Maggie probably had that in hand.

U think he's ok? I asked.

Probably. I just wanted to let you know he'll be back late.

I tried to go back to my studying, but I was thoroughly distracted, first wondering if he was going to be okay, and then wondering why I cared so much. It wasn't like we even liked each other.

He didn't return until almost midnight. He hobbled into the room on crutches, his foot bandaged all to hell, but there was no cast. "It's not broken?" I asked instead of saying hello.

Maggie helped him hop over to his bed. "No," he said. "Sprained ankle and a broken toe. Which hurts like a mother."

"Doctor's orders are to stay off of his leg as much as he can and to keep it elevated," said Maggie. "But he should be back to normal in a few weeks."

"Okay." I wasn't sure why Maggie was telling me this. Was I his nurse now?

Maggie shrugged and turned her attention back on Peter. She moved him around on the bed until she got his foot propped up on some pillows. He kept swatting at her hands, clearly uncomfortable, but she continued to mother him anyway, even asking if he wanted something to drink.

Exasperated, he said, "I'm fine. I just want to take one of those pain pills and pass out."

She threw up her hands. "Fine." She fished in her messenger bag and came back with a white paper bag that had a prescription slip stapled to it. She handed it to him. "Text me tomorrow when you need to get to class."

"I will. Thanks, Maggie."

She frowned. "Are you sure you're okay?"

"I'll be fine. Logan's here, so it's not like I'm alone. Go home to your boyfriend. I'll text you in the morning."

She nodded. "Okay. See you tomorrow."

When she was gone, Peter groaned. "Sorry. I assume you heard what happened?"

"Ellie texted me."

He nodded. "Maggie called my parents and they threatened to drive all the way out here. I think I managed to talk them out of that, but I can't believe Maggie called them."

I considered making an argument on his parents' behalf, but I completely understood. My own mother would have just spent the whole time hounding the doctor for information, and my father probably would have lectured me on how injuring myself could very well end my violin career. "I get it," I said instead.

"Could you grab me a soda from the fridge?"

As I got up to walk over to our little minifridge, he said, "Yeah, so, the fall wasn't so far, maybe three or four feet, but I landed on my left foot all wrong. It's a pretty bad sprain and I broke my pinkie toe to boot, so it hurts, but it's not the worst. I really thought my foot was broken for a while there."

I handed him a can of soda. "Yeah, I sprained my ankle a few years ago. It's no picnic."

"They couldn't do much for me besides wrap a bandage around my ankle and tape up my toes. So I have to keep it wrapped and minimize how much weight I put on it for a few weeks. Hence the crutches." He sighed and pulled a medicine bottle out of the paper bag. He twisted off the top. "The doctor was nice enough to give me some pain drugs, at least, so no offense, but my plan really is to take one and pass the hell out and forget this whole night ever happened."

"Sounds like a good plan."

I left him to it and went back to my desk. Studying wasn't happening, but I pretended to look at my sheet music while I was still aware of him behind me. He kept moving around, and I glanced back in time to see him wriggle out of his jeans while trying to keep his leg elevated. He had on dark red briefs under the jeans, and I realized that he'd never been naked enough around me for me to have gleaned his underwear preferences. I was also super turned on, because those red briefs stretched tautly over his—*Jesus*.

"You need help?" I asked before I could stop myself.

He succeeded in freeing his feet of his pants and tossed them at his desk. They landed on his chair. "Nah, I got it." He jostled around some more until he was half under his covers, the injured foot still propped up above the covers on those pillows. Once he was settled, he banged his head back against his pillows and said, "Christ."

"Let me know if you need something."

"Thanks, bro."

Bro? Really?

I sighed and turned back to my homework. After a few minutes of pretending to study, I got up to go brush my teeth. Peter was dead to the world.

CHAPTER 7

BASICALLY IF I wasn't at class or rehearsal, I was studying, because I had to maintain a certain GPA to keep my scholarship, no matter how talented I was. Thus I was starting to snooze over my laptop—"studying"—when Peter hobbled in the next afternoon. Once he was inside, he kicked the door closed, threw himself face-first onto the bed, and grunted into his pillow.

"Rough day?" I asked.

He rolled onto his back. "It's bad enough that pretty much everything on my left leg from about midshin down hurts like hell. But Maggie's piece-of-shit car broke down this morning. She had to get it towed. It won't be fixed for at least a week. I had to walk back from Dickinson, which I do *not* recommend doing on crutches." He let out a pained breath. "Holy fuck that hurts."

"I'm sorry," I said for lack of anything better.

He rolled slowly and sat up. "Hey, you have a car."

Oh, no. "I do, yes." I did *not* want to play chauffeur for the next few weeks. I could barely stay on top of everything I had to do as it was. "But our schedules are really incompatible. Don't you have someone with a more similar schedule who can help you around? What about your girlfriend?"

He tilted his head and furrowed his brow. "My girlfriend?"

"Yeah." Didn't he know he had a girlfriend? "That girl Lily you hang around with all the time."

He laughed. "Oh, dude, no. Lily is not my girlfriend."

I sat on my bed across from him. "Sorry. You guys seem awfully handsy with each other. I just assumed."

He nodded, as if that made sense, but he'd never considered it before. "Anyway, no. Lily doesn't have a car. None of my friends do. Well, Dave does, but he lives off campus." He held out his hands. "I know this is a big thing to ask, but it would really help me, and it's only for a few days—a week at most—until I can get around better. If you could just, like, get me to the middle of campus in the morning and pick me up at the end of the day, even, that would be a big help."

"All right," I said, not willing to be the asshole who left him in the lurch. "I guess I can manage that."

His face went bright with gratitude. "Thank you. I'll make it up to you somehow. I'll pay for your next gas refill and buy you dinner or something. And not even at the Mac, somewhere in town."

"Okay." I wasn't sure how I'd do with him one-on-one through a meal. We got along okay in the room, but mostly if we were both home, one or both of us was studying, so it wasn't like we had a lot of social time. He was clearly trying to engage me, but I was resistant. Would we even have enough to say to each other to sustain conversation through a whole dinner? Was I overthinking this?

"Thanks, Logan. I really mean it."

Heat rose to my face, and I shook my head. "It's no problem."

IT *WAS* kind of a problem, though. I knew I was being an asshole by not wanting to drive Peter to class. I should have been a friend, or at least a nice guy, by helping him out. But my schedule was unworkable as it was. Not to mention he annoyed me *so much*. His stupid sexy, perky ways, dampened somewhat by the recent injury, were like that first step into sunlight after being inside all day, bright and searing.

But I decided to suck it up. That afternoon, after he asked me to be his driver, he said he was done with class for the day, plus it was *Piper Hill* night with Lily, so I drove myself to orchestra rehearsal, still seething a little.

Rehearsal was… fine.

First Costner gave us a new piece of music to learn, a Beethoven concerto I was familiar with. Based on how badly the orchestra butchered it while trying to sight-read, I suspected most of the rest of the musicians had never heard it before. After fifteen minutes of trying to play through the first movement, Costner said, "No, no, no. The key is C *minor*. Three flats. You're all playing A flat and E flat too sharp. C minor is supposed to sound dark and stormy. Emotional. Not like a little dance ditty. Half steps, violins. Do it again."

We moved on to the Bach we'd been working on all semester. Costner had me play my solo when it came up as we played through the song, but then he kept cutting me off and saying, "It's fine, Logan. It's fine. Measure one fifty-four!" This was the cue to skip right over my parts of the piece and to the parts the rest of the orchestra came in on.

But according to Costner, this was all wrong too. "*D* minor now. A and E are natural now. Everything is too flat. And it's messy, second violins. Clean it up."

We played the same three lines of music eight times, until Costner seemed satisfied, but then he turned toward the second violins again. "We wouldn't have had to waste time with that if you all practiced more. This isn't a jam session. I expect you to come to rehearsal prepared. You need to have this down by next week, okay?"

I liked Costner most of the time. He wasn't usually this hostile. He was a good, if demanding, teacher. But now I wanted to pull him aside to point out that he'd chosen music that was beyond what most of the students could play. But he persisted, and by the end of rehearsal, we were sounding better as a group, and he said, "See that? I knew you could get it. Violins, watch out for those half steps. See you next week."

The moment rehearsal ended and Costner dismissed us, he walked over to me and said, "You were a little off with timing today."

"I was?"

He lifted his baton and started waving it to show upbeats and downbeats. "I know you know how to do this, Logan. Keep up with me. I don't know if you could hear it from up here in front, but you were half a beat off the baton on that last go through, but the last row of violins must have been following your bow, because the sound wasn't quite holding together."

"Got it. Sorry about that."

"Not a problem. Get it right next time. Can you come to the second violin sectional on Friday afternoon? You don't have a class at three, do you?"

"No, I don't. The *second* violin sectional?"

"I want to go over the key signatures with them again. You can colead the sectional with me and Nancy." Nancy was the second violin section leader. "I'll send you an e-mail with what I want to cover."

"Okay," I said. As the concertmaster, I had among my responsibilities to lead violin sectionals. I was, essentially, the orchestra leader, kind of like a captain, so teaching sectionals was something I'd been doing all semester, but usually I worked with the first violins. I didn't mind another rehearsal so much as I already missed the downtime I'd have had Friday afternoon.

Costner patted my shoulder and told me to have a good night.

As I packed up, Ellie walked over. "Guess what," she said.

"It's Tater Tot day at the dining hall?"

"Oh, if only." Ellie looked off into the distance as if she were imagining such a great and wonderful time. "No, I have two important pieces of news. Neither of which is violin-related."

"Good. I've had enough violin for today. What's up?"

"Rachel finally dumped her horrible boyfriend. I think for good this time."

"That's good. Is she back to normal?"

Ellie smirked. "In between bouts of weeping, yes."

"What was your other piece of news?"

"I totally killed the midterm in my lit class."

My relief for her was palpable. Ellie had spent much of the previous week fretting about that exam. "Congrats!"

"No grades yet, but I knew the info on the test cold. Seriously, ask me anything about nineteenth-century British lit. I know it.

Symbolism in *Wuthering Heights*, the belief system of the pre-Raphaelites, how crazy Lord Byron was, the domestic politics of Jane Austen, I got it all up here." She tapped the side of her head.

I had to look around for the little rosin cake that lived in my violin case, since it wasn't in its pocket, but I said, "That's awesome," as I looked. It was on the music stand.

"How's your poor injured roommate?" Ellie asked.

I grimaced. "He asked me to drive him around campus. I guess Maggie's car broke down."

Ellie let out a burst of laughter. "What did you say to that?"

"I agreed. Not like I had a choice."

"Wow. He really gets your goat, doesn't he? What is it about this guy?"

I picked up my case and slung it over my shoulder before grabbing my music folder and shoving it in my bag. "I don't know. He's annoying. He's hot. I find the combination of these two things super desirable, apparently."

She pointed at me. "I knew it!"

We walked out of the orchestra room and toward the staircase that led back to the parking lot. "Don't plan the wedding yet," I said. "Sure, I'm attracted to him. He's also straight and my roommate. And even if he were gay, which he isn't, it's not like I could make a move on him without fucking up my housing situation more than it already is."

"Valid," said Ellie. "You going back up the hill?"

"Yeah. Want a ride?"

"Sure, thanks." She elbowed me. "See how easy that was?"

I groaned as we got to my car. I had to fish the remote starter out of my pocket and get our instruments carefully arranged in the backseat, but once I was behind the wheel, she said, "He *is* pretty cute."

"Can we not?"

"See, I kind of figured the reason he annoyed you so much is because you secretly like him. You're acting about as mature as the boy on the playground who pulls on the girl's pigtails. Maybe you should make a move."

"And get punched in the face? No, thank you." I put the car in gear.

"Peter would never punch anybody. And he could be into dudes. You don't know. Stop being a child."

"Trust me, my interest in Peter is not childish." A sudden mental image of him wriggling out of his jeans, with those powerful thighs and the bulge in his little red briefs, made me feel flush all over. "But it's not like I like him as a person. He's still annoying. This is all just lust."

"There's something kind of sexy about the situation, isn't there? He's your roommate. Maybe he comes back from the shower one afternoon and drops his towel…."

Ugh. "No. You should watch less gay porn."

"Or now he's injured, you could Florence Nightingale him back to health, and when it's over, he'll be ever so grateful…."

Heat washed over me, but I shook my head. "Forget it. He would never."

"He's really not so bad. He's kind of anal about backstage theater stuff, sure, but he seems like a nice guy. Half the girls in Theater Club are in love with him."

"They can have him."

I drove up the hill, and Ellie was silent for a few minutes, but when I pulled into the parking lot behind Emerson, she said, "I guess I don't really know him that well, but from what I've seen at *Oklahoma!* rehearsals this semester, he doesn't seem as bad as you say."

"Can we not talk about this anymore?"

She pulled her violin case out of the backseat. "Sure. I have to study anyway. I killed one midterm, but I have two more to go. See ya!"

She blew me a kiss and walked toward her dorm.

I got my own stuff out of the car and trudged back to my room. Rehearsal had run long, so I wasn't that surprised to find Peter by himself, snoozing on his bed. Thankfully, he was wearing pajama pants this time.

God, he was beautiful.

But, no, I was moving on with my life. I had a music theory final to study for. I put my violin away and got out my book and tried to ignore his gentle snoring.

CHAPTER 8

THURSDAY MORNINGS Peter and I both had class in Dickinson Hall. It was easy walking distance from our dorm if you didn't have a sprained ankle. The small parking lots near the academic buildings were often battlefields where faculty and extremely lucky students competed for the rare empty spots, so it wasn't worth it to drive. But Peter had come through with a coveted red parking pass on account of his injury. The red pass meant I could park my car pretty much wherever I wanted on campus.

Unfortunately I still had to get to the magical red-pass-only parking lot right across the street from Dickinson. And traffic that morning was especially epic, the roads through campus packed with slow drivers as if everyone in Western Massachusetts had decided a morning drive was just the thing.

"What class do you have today?" Peter asked as we idled at a traffic light.

Small talk? That was how this was going to go? All right. "Twentieth Century American Lit," I said. "I figure I should take at least one nonmusic class per semester. You?"

"Income tax." He sighed. "Don't laugh."

"I'm not laughing. That sounds dreadful."

"It is."

When I glanced at him before driving through the traffic stop, he was gazing out the window.

"I mean," he said after we passed through the intersection, "I don't know how much longer I can do this. I hate these classes so much."

"Why are you majoring in accounting, then?"

"My father's a CPA. I'm supposed to go into the family business when I finish college."

"Sure. I get that." I probably knew better than anyone about the weight of parental expectations.

"I'm pretty good at math and whatever, but I never wanted to be an accountant."

Who would? "What do you want to be?"

"Honestly? I kind of wanted to go to art school."

I balked. That surprised the hell out of me. "Really?"

"Yeah. Like, graphic design or something. I mean, I love to paint. That's why I like to do the scenery for the Theater Club so much. But I like all kinds of art. I don't know." Peter sighed again. "I envy you, you know that? You get to study music, just like you've always wanted. My parents would never let me do that. 'The arts are totally impractical.'" He said the last part in a deeper voice, as if he were imitating someone, probably his father.

I wanted to interrupt him to tell him my parents had actually pressured me into the violin major and that I had some serious doubts too. I suspected my desire to play violin forever was about at the same level as Peter's desire to be an accountant. I opened my mouth to say something to that effect, but he wasn't done.

"God," he said. "Of course, I can't go to art school because that's a gay thing to do."

I was so surprised by the comment that I almost missed the turn into the parking lot. My tires squealed as I took the turn too hard, which forced Peter to throw his arms out and brace himself against the glove compartment.

"Jesus," he whispered.

"Sorry." But I wasn't sorry. I was pissed. Art school was gay? What the hell was that supposed to mean? And art school? Did Peter like art? He'd been excited about painting those sets for the Theater Club—his busted ankle was a sacrifice to those sets, after all—but he'd never struck me as being an art fan. The decorations on his side of our room were so generic—rock posters and such—that I wondered suddenly if he thought all art was gay. I squeezed the steering wheel, trying to keep a lid on my anger.

I didn't get a chance to ask Peter about any of it, because there was a prize parking spot right near the crosswalk, so I took it. He must have guessed I was upset, because he got right out of the car and retrieved his crutches from the backseat.

"Are you mad?" he asked. "Because I didn't mean—"

"Forget it." I didn't want to hear his feeble excuses for saying shitty homophobic things. "You need a hand getting across the street?"

He hopped forward on the crutches a couple of paces. "I think I got it. But maybe spot me until we get to the building?"

"All right."

But I wasn't any less mad by the time I saw him into Dickinson and we parted ways.

He must have known I was gay. I wondered again if he didn't. It was possible. It wasn't like I was dating anyone or had posters of hot guys on the walls of my dorm room. Well, I'd put a photo of my current celebrity crush—this bulky blond actor who had been in a bunch of indie movies and was totally dead sexy—as the background on my laptop, which Peter borrowed periodically because his computer was old and constantly on the fritz. So he'd seen that. I doubted straight guys had photos of hot blond actors as their desktop background.

But… wait, maybe he didn't know. Maybe he thought I'd agree with his opinions.

Still, it was hardly appropriate to disparage artistic pursuits as being gay. Maybe that was why he did tech but didn't sing himself. As if building sets was more macho than acting or whatever the fuck. Maybe it was better for me to hear his unvarnished opinion than whatever he would have said if he'd thought enough to censor himself. So I had come back around to mad again by the time I slipped behind a desk in my English class.

Despite traffic, I was still about five minutes early and the professor wasn't there yet. My friend Fred came in and sat next to me. He said, "If you keep staring like that, laser beams will come out of your eyes."

I grunted.

He scoffed. "Who pissed in your cornflakes this morning?"

I glanced at Fred. He was surprisingly dressed down today, wearing a gray T-shirt and jeans; the one nod to his usual aesthetic was a pair of bright red suspenders. Fred had been born about fifty years too late. Often he looked like he belonged on a stage reciting poetry at a bar during the beat era, and he liked to quote Jack Kerouac. We'd become friends when he'd hit on me by inviting me to his apartment to smoke a joint and listen to Miles Davis records. So we'd had that one date, which didn't really go anywhere. I liked him as a friend, but he was super pretentious.

I said, "My roommate called me gay."

Fred leaned over and put a hand on my desk. He looked at me with mock gravity. "I have bad news for you. You *are* gay."

I rolled my eyes. "No, I mean, he said studying the arts in college was a gay thing to do. In the bad way. In the *gay* as a synonym for *lame* or *stupid* way."

"Ah. That jerk."

"I know. Stupid Housing. I hate this guy, but it's too late to change."

"Yeah, been there. My roommate freshman year was this total dickhead homophobic asshole who made a sport of picking on me, and usually he got his friends involved too. That's why I moved off campus."

I didn't think Peter was an asshole, and he'd never actually made fun of me. Until today, that was. But I said, "I guess I could look into that for senior year."

"Lots of cheap apartments in this town. My place is a dump, but at least I don't have to share it. Oh, and Noel—you know Noel, right, from the Queer Student Union?"

I had forgotten that Fred regularly went to QSU meetings. If I had any hope of ever having sex again, I should probably have started going too. If not for my stupid Tuesday night rehearsal. But that was neither here nor there. "I know Noel."

"He's dating some guy off campus. Told me his boyfriend's apartment is really nice. It's that apartment complex in North Amherst near the gas station? Past the high school?"

I knew of it. "Okay."

"It's an option, is what I'm saying. If you can swing it, it sure as hell beats the dorms."

"I will definitely think about it." I glanced around the room. Still no professor and everyone was chatting, so I said, "How is the QSU these days?"

Fred shrugged. "Fine. I only go to, like, every other meeting. There are a bunch of new people this year, which is cool. And that smoking hot guy from last year is back. His name never stays in my head, though. He speaks and all I hear are angels singing. His name is Paul, maybe?"

"Okay."

"And Noel's boyfriend is pretty active. I guess he just came out over the summer, so he's all gung ho about getting involved."

I knew guys like that. I found it charming.

"You should come to a meeting, though," Fred said. "That jerk Simon finally graduated."

"I have a violin class at the same time you guys meet." I'd even checked my schedule to verify the meeting time after Ellie lectured me about not doing anything social this semester. I really didn't have time. My dick was going to wither and fall off.

"Oh. Right. Well, maybe next semester. Now that Simon's gone, the meetings are a lot more fun."

"Sure. Maybe."

The professor strolled in then and apologized for being late. Talking to Fred had diffused some of my anger, and I was generally able to pay attention to the discussion on *The Sound and the Fury* the class was engaged in, but every now and then my mind would drift off toward stupid, annoying, sexy Peter.

What a goddamned mess.

AFTER CLASS, I had an appointment with my advisor. My anger had dissipated somewhat while my classmates debated about whether some of Faulkner's characters were offensive, and I tried to focus on the bigger matter at hand, which was that I had a decision to make.

My advisor, Professor Schuler, was a flautist who taught music theory and a few other classes. Unlike Costner, she never pushed me. We met once a semester, during which time she mostly reviewed the requirements for my music performance major with me and made sure I'd get all the classes in before I graduated.

Butterflies flitted around my stomach as I walked down the hall to her office because I'd decided to present her with the hypothetical question of whether I should even continue with the major, and I had no idea how she'd receive that. I'd been flirting with the idea for a few weeks, of changing course so that I could make more time in my life for things that weren't the violin, wondering how my life would be different if I weren't a concert violinist. At this point, the idea was just a fantasy I had late at night when I couldn't sleep, but I thought it worth broaching the subject with my advisor.

She had an office at the end of a long hallway in Hawthorne Hall, which was where a lot of the nonperformance music classes met. Walking down that hallway felt like walking down a gauntlet. I kept expecting big men with swords to jump out at me and attack.

Professor Schuler looked up with a smile when I rapped on the frame of her door. "Logan! Good to see you. Come in."

As I sat in the chair across her desk from her and found a little spot for my bag in her tiny, crowded office, she did something on her computer, probably pulling up my academic record.

"How's your semester going?" she asked. "Professor Costner said you're playing a Bach solo in the December concert."

"Oh. Yeah, I am. This semester has been… busy. That's kind of why I wanted to talk to you."

"Sure. Let me just… okay." She clicked her mouse a few times. "Registration for next semester is still a few weeks away, but the schedule is out, so I can try to work out what you should take. You still need one more semester of music theory and apparently musical arrangement…. I thought you took arrangement already?"

"I took Arrangement 1 sophomore year and I'm taking composition right now. But before we—"

"Yeah, okay. I see that. So, Arrangement 2, for sure, and then Music History and Culture. Between that and all your private instruction and ensemble requirements, that's your semester, basically. Unless you want to take an elective?"

"Oh. Well, maybe. I hadn't thought about it. I wanted to talk about something else."

She finally looked away from her computer. "Okay. What's up?"

I took a deep breath. "Well, see, and this is just hypothetical, but say you had a student who had finished five semesters of a music performance major and now maybe doesn't want to be a musician. As a career, I mean."

She looked at me for a long moment, and then her face softened. "Are you having second thoughts?"

"I just… I don't know. Say I wanted to teach instead of perform. How would that affect the rest of my time here?"

Professor Schuler frowned. She tapped the stack of textbooks on her desk. "Just hypothetically, that's at least another year of school. You'd have to take all the education requirements plus two semesters of student teaching. You could do some of the coursework and the student teaching at the same time, but I wouldn't really recommend it. Are you really thinking of changing majors?"

She sounded so disappointed that I wanted to say, "Ha-ha, just kidding," and run out of there, but instead I took a deep breath and said, "This can't leave this room. I haven't decided anything yet."

"No, of course. We're just talking. We don't have to decide anything today."

"Right. I just keep thinking about what you said when I was a freshman. That this major was really for people who wanted to make music their career. I thought I did two years ago, but I'm less sure now. And shouldn't I have a career to fall back on in case I don't get into a big orchestra?"

"There are a lot of paths for you, Logan." She leaned forward a little. "I completely hear what you're saying, and I understand.

Here's my recommendation. Go ahead and finish the performance major. You're already a junior, and we generally don't recommend changing majors this late in the game. If next year you still want to teach, there are a lot of graduate programs that accept students who didn't study education as an undergrad. You can get a master's in music education, which a lot of states require now anyway. That's also more school, but this way you have options. Maybe play in an orchestra for a few years and come back to teaching later. Maybe do something else entirely. Yeah?"

I let out a breath. It seemed like something I could do. Three more semesters of performance, and then if I wanted to do something else, I could go to grad school. My grades were strong enough that there would be a lot of possibilities. "That seems reasonable."

Professor Schuler smiled. "You're young. Nothing is set in stone. Okay? Now, about next semester...."

Now that the hard part of the appointment was over, I basically just said yes to whatever Professor Schuler recommended, and my mind wandered back to Peter. He wasn't studying for his ideal career either, but what really kept him from pursuing what he wanted? Some fear of being branded gay?

His words from that morning echoed in my head, and I was angry all over again. By the time the appointment wrapped up, it was all I could do not to snap at Professor Schuler that I'd take the dumb music history class already. Instead I summoned all my patience while she printed the list of classes she wanted me to register for, and I forced a smile when she handed it to me. I shoved the paper in my bag as I ran back up to my dorm, because if I didn't hustle, I'd be late for rehearsal.

And didn't that feel like the story of my life?

CHAPTER 9

THE SPRAIN was bad enough that Peter still couldn't put weight on his ankle by the time the next Theater Club rehearsal rolled around. He was still in charge of set design and the tech crew, so that meant he'd be there late, and he'd asked me to pick him up afterward. Just to make me feel more like a heel, it coincided with when my extra session with Professor Costner let out, so I was already on campus—picking him up was hardly an imposition.

And yet I still resented him for the "gay" comment. Ellie told me I was being petty, and maybe I was, but it pissed me off so much that I'd been mostly avoiding him for the past few days. As he was largely confined to our building if he didn't have help getting around, that was an easy enough accomplishment. We mostly only interacted at night, or when I drove him to and from the center of campus.

I pulled up to the curb to wait for him. I must have been early, because usually after rehearsal, there were a bunch of people hanging out behind Burroughs Auditorium. Some students waited for rides, some lit up cigarettes, most just lingered chatting before dispersing to go to their dorms or apartments. But no one was there when I cut the engine to my car. Well, there was one guy standing there, leaning against a banged-up old sedan also parked at the curb.

I got out of my car. It was a damp night, though it wasn't raining just then. I really wanted a cigarette, but I'd kicked that over the summer, so I didn't have any on me. This guy didn't look like he would either.

"Hey," I said to the guy, an athletic type in a Red Sox cap. "Rehearsal's not out yet?"

He looked up from his phone. "Oh. No. Running late."

Wanting the company, I walked over. He looked vaguely familiar. Maybe I'd just seen him around campus or he was also in the music program or something. "I'm picking up my roommate," I volunteered. "He hurt his foot last week."

"Is your roommate Peter?"

I realized I knew this guy because I'd seen him hanging out with Peter; he was one of Peter's jock friends. "Yeah," I said, feeling on guard now.

The guy looked me up and down in a way I found creepy and disturbing, but then he smirked. "I thought you'd be taller."

I had no idea what that was supposed to mean, so I turned back toward the building entrance. "Ha-ha, everyone make fun of the small guy."

"Hey, did I make fun? No. Just… Peter has mentioned you, but in his descriptions, you sound… bigger than you are. Or I was just picturing a taller guy, I don't know. Forget I said anything. I didn't mean it." He looked me over again. "He was right, though. You do have a short fuse."

"The fuck? You guys talk about me?"

The guy opened his mouth to speak but then shut it again and shrugged. "You're Logan, right? I'm Dave."

"All right."

Dave tilted his head. "Look, don't get offended. All I meant was that Peter has brought you up in conversation a few times. Not in a bad way. Just, you know, 'Logan's a violinist,' or 'Logan's giving me a ride to rehearsal.' That kind of thing."

He was clearly trying to disarm me, so I took a deep breath and tried to let my anger go. "Sorry. He's just… I'm not his biggest fan right at the moment. I just want to pick him up and go back to my room so I can finish studying for the exam I have tomorrow."

"Why *aren't* you his biggest fan? Because Peter's a pretty great guy."

I took a turn looking Dave over. He was wearing a faded blue T-shirt and dark jeans, nothing eye-catching, and his brown hair curled out from under his baseball cap. He was cute, actually, but also sort of nondescript. He looked relaxed, like he didn't give a shit whether anyone noticed him. Probably because he was parked there waiting for his undemanding girlfriend.

"He said something the other day that offended me," I said, figuring I'd keep it vague.

Dave laughed. "Really? What was it?"

"You wouldn't understand."

Dave grinned. "Try me. Peter's a sweetheart, but he puts his foot in his mouth sometimes, so I get it."

What an odd thing to say. Had I missed some weird step in evolution where straight guys referred to each other as *sweetheart*? "Well, if you must know, he said something kind of homophobic."

Dave stared at me for a long moment, his eyebrows raised. "Homophobic? Peter? Are we talking about the same guy?"

"You know a lot of other Peters with sprained ankles?"

"No. But... Peter is...."

I waved my hand while he stumbled over what to say to placate me. "Maybe he didn't mean it to be homophobic, but it was. You'd never understand, though. You straight guys say things all the time without realizing how they might come across to someone who isn't straight."

"Ah," Dave said. "I think I see the problem here."

I couldn't wait for this explanation. I crossed my arms. "I'll bite."

"Okay, first of all, maybe turn the rage down to, like, a five? No need to have it set to eleven."

I took a deep breath. I supposed I had sounded kind of hostile. "Fine. Sorry."

"Great. Second of all, you should know, I'm here to pick up my *boyfriend*. Noel? He's playing Will Parker."

I stared at Dave for a long minute, agog. What Dave was telling me did not compute. This guy was gay? And dating Noel? Pretty boy Noel? After hearing about Noel's amazing boyfriend all semester, this guy was the last person I imagined Noel with, but I believed him. "Oh. Yeah, I know Noel."

"Don't make snap judgments, is what I'm saying. And as for Peter, well, do you want to know how I know him?"

I shrugged. "You had a class together?"

"No. I met him at a Queer Student Union meeting."

This was all too much. "What the hell was Peter doing—"

"It's probably not even my place to tell you this, but he's gay. Like, card-carrying, active in the QSU, seems to have a thing for gothy twinks, out to pretty much everyone gay. Although apparently he never came out to you, if by some chance you didn't know. But anyway, this is why I seriously doubt he said anything homophobic and meant it. Maybe you misheard, or he was joking and you didn't realize it. But I can't imagine Peter saying anything remotely hateful."

Was that what had happened? I thought back on his comment. He'd been saying that he'd wanted to go to art school but couldn't because it was too gay. I'd been offended by that, but what was he really saying? That art school was too gay for Peter or too gay for his parents? Given the context of the conversation, in retrospect, he must have meant the latter.

"Oh my God."

"Yeah," said Dave.

I was prevented from speaking more because the doors burst open and the Theater Club kids all spilled out.

If I'd had any doubts about Dave's sexuality, they were quickly assuaged. A huge grin bloomed across his face as Noel barreled toward him. Noel threw himself at Dave and Dave caught him. Then Dave kissed him. And kissed him. And *kissed him*. I looked away, embarrassed.

When they finished making out, Noel said, "It's good to see you," and I turned back.

Dave glanced at me. "Yeah, sorry. I know I've been working a lot lately…."

Noel seemed to recognize that he'd interrupted a conversation. He turned toward me and waved. "Hi, Logan. Sorry. You here to pick up Peter?"

"Yeah, I…."

"I see you met my boyfriend." Noel beamed at Dave again.

I turned and looked back toward the doors, hoping to spontaneously combust. It certainly felt like I was about to catch fire, given how hot my face felt. The man himself emerged then, propelling himself forward on his crutches, a girl walking next to him, carrying his backpack. Not his girlfriend, clearly. Because he was gay. And I was a jerk.

He smiled when he saw me. "Hi. Thanks."

"Of course." I took the backpack from the girl.

Peter looked between me and Dave. "I see you've all met. Ah, Ashley, this is my roommate-slash-chauffeur, Logan."

Ashley was vaguely familiar, with a lot of curly hair. She offered her hand for shaking. "Nice to meet you."

We stood around for a moment. I felt awkward as Peter greeted Dave and made small talk. It became clear pretty quickly, though, that Peter was tired, and the way he kept shifting his weight on the crutches indicated he was uncomfortable. So I intervened on his behalf and even did him a solid by playing the jerk. "Hey, we should get going. I've got a lot of homework tonight."

He shot me a grateful look, his eyebrows slightly raised.

We were both quiet as I drove us back up the hill to our dorm. The magical parking pass meant I could park in the lot closest to our dorm, otherwise reserved for the residential staff, and I found a spot in the little lot a few feet from the back of the building. As I parked, Peter said, "I'm going to the doctor tomorrow to see if I can lose the crutches. Lily's borrowing her roommate's car to drive me."

"Okay."

"So probably this is the last time you'll have to drive me around. The foot feels all right. I think the bruises under my arms from the crutches hurt more."

"Sure." I'd known this moment was coming—I'd been looking forward to being relieved of this particular obligation—but in light of what I now knew, I was… disappointed. We would no longer have our car rides to talk inside our private bubble. Not that our room wasn't also a bubble of sorts, but there was something about the two of us in my car that felt special, in retrospect.

On the other hand, I wouldn't have to drive him around anymore. His injured foot was no longer my problem. Right?

"I mean, thanks," Pater said. "I really appreciate your going out of your way to help me."

"You're welcome." I turned off the car and just sat for a moment, waiting to see if he'd say something more.

He got out of the car.

I helped him back to the room. He put his stuff away and then tossed the crutches at his desk. He lay on his bed.

So quiet was how we were doing things.

He flipped on the TV and changed the channel to some superhero show before settling into his pillow. Taking my cue, I grabbed a book and sat at my desk, pretending to study while sitting with the information that my smoking hot roommate was gay. I supposed that didn't make him immune to being homophobic, but as I sat there and reexamined every interaction we'd had all semester, I realized how much I'd misjudged him. Hell, he'd been trying to befriend me for a couple of months, hadn't he? Instead I'd treated him like he had the plague.

God.

I turned to say something—I wasn't sure what, an apology of some sorts maybe—and saw he'd passed out on the bed, his mouth slightly ajar. Feeling some strange affection for him, and knowing it would get cold in the room when the heat went off in the wee hours of the morning, I grabbed his extra blanket and covered him with it. He stirred slightly and snorted but settled immediately back into sleep.

And I was left wondering what the hell I was supposed to do now.

CHAPTER 10

I SPENT a week at stealthy reconnaissance.

On Monday, after a particularly dull music theory class, I hiked up the hill to my dorm and managed to catch Peter in our room before he left for *Oklahoma!* rehearsal. He was on the phone when I came in, and he frowned and stared at the ceiling, clenching his teeth a lot, so clearly this was not a pleasant conversation. He didn't say much, mostly communicated in monosyllables.

"Parents?" I mouthed.

He nodded. Then he told the caller, "Dad. Dad, stop it. I sent the application in. They're not telling people for another few weeks. We just have to wait."

Things went on in this vein for a while, so I tried to ignore him—never possible, but I could kid myself—and then I couldn't find the folder of music I needed for that night's orchestra rehearsal and spent a good while ransacking the room. Peter apparently found this hilarious, because he pulled the phone away from his head and said, "Hey, knock it off," with a giggle in his voice.

I found the folder—somehow it had slid under my bed— around the same time he got off the phone. He groaned and tossed his phone at his bed, where it landed with a thud on the bedspread.

"My family is exhausting," he said.

"I hear you. My father called yesterday to tell me he'd seen a PBS special with some orchestra in London that premiered a new piece of music, and it wasn't enough for me to play for the orchestra, I should be concentrating on composition as well, as if anyone who doesn't write movie scores makes money at classical music anymore."

"High expectations, huh?"

"The *highest.*"

We had a moment where we both nodded in solidarity, but it passed quickly. I wanted to say something, but my mind went blank, so I just sat there, trying not to stare at him. Peter stood, picked up his backpack, and said, "I better get going to rehearsal. See you later, Logan." He limped out of the room. He hobbled around on his own now, recovered enough that he no longer needed a ride around campus.

On Tuesday, between my last class and trying to whip the first violins into shape at our sectional rehearsal, I went to the Mac to grab dinner. I spotted Peter eating with Dave and Noel and some guy with a lot of piercings whom I'd never seen before. Pierced guy was wearing a "Some people are gay. Get over it." T-shirt, so I had a guess for how they all knew each other. Said guy was also super flirty with Peter, which made rage boil up in me something fierce.

I recognized my brief bout of insanity as jealousy, which was stupid because Peter and I weren't dating, and he probably didn't even like me much since I'd been an asshole to him all semester. I hightailed it out of the Mac before he could see me.

I knew where a few of Peter's classes were from my time as his chauffeur, so I took the long way to all of my Wednesday classes with the hopes of seeing him. No dice, but then on my way to the FAC for my music composition class, I spotted him outside Dickinson Hall, cracking up with a couple of girls I recognized from the Theater Club. They moved in a way that was so animated, I figured they must have been reenacting part of a play. One of the girls broke into song—I was too far away to hear what it was, but her voice rang through the air—and Peter laughed and clapped and was clearly delighted. After class that day, I took the elevator into the bowels of the FAC and practiced/hid in a practice room for a couple of hours, because now I felt like a stalker. I played Bach until my fingers hurt and the furious cloud of bow rosin I'd kicked up made me a little sniffly.

I had an early class Thursday, so I didn't see Peter until the end of the day, when I stopped by the room to grab my violin before my one-on-one class with Costner. Then there he was, on the other side of the quad, and he was clearly on his way to the gym, probably for the first time since getting off his crutches. He high-fived some dude on the way. After my time with Costner, I had a brief break before I had to go back to the FAC to help out with another violin sectional, so Ellie dragged me to the dining hall to force dinner on me. And there was Peter, across the room, chatting with Lily and apparently making some kind of sculpture out of the dining hall's very cheap, bendable flatware.

I had given up stalking him by Friday, because I could no longer remember why I was so obsessed, but then I saw him standing in line to check out some books at the library, and he gave me a cute little wave before turning to flirt with the guy working the circulation desk. Oh, right. He was smoking hot. And gay. And I was looking for proof of that, I supposed, and also evidence that I'd misjudged him, which I most definitely had.

Most of what I learned during my week of spying was that Peter was hot and everyone liked him. He was clearly a shameless flirt, and I'd been too blinded by my own stupidity to notice. He had a ton of friends, and he kept busy both academically and socially. By the end of the week, I wasn't jealous so much as feeling really terrible about myself, because he had all these people around him all the time, and I had… music.

Friday night I had dinner in town with Ellie. We squeezed into a booth in Amherst Center's crowded burrito place, always packed because it had the best food in town. The counter had a line at least ten people deep and growing, so I felt pretty grateful to have a seat.

As I worked out how best to bite into a burrito the size of a cantaloupe, Ellie said, "So your boy Peter had an op-ed published in *The Minuteman*." She handed me a copy of the school paper already folded over to show the editorial page.

"He's not my boy." He probably wouldn't even be my roommate much longer, at the rate we were going, since I'd been avoiding him all week while also spying on him. And I wasn't really that stealthy, so he probably thought I was a creeper now. I took the paper. "What's the editorial about?"

"Apparently Student Activities wants to kill the LGBT semiformal, because we live in a post-homophobic society where LGBT people are completely accepted, so there's no need for a separate dance."

How absurd. "Right."

"Anyway, Peter wrote an editorial arguing we still need it because some kids don't feel safe being out on campus. Apparently there was some incident at the Mac a couple of weeks ago in which there was a confrontation between some football jocks and the Theater Club kids."

"Wow, really? I didn't hear about that."

"Luckily it didn't amount to much more than name-calling."

I glanced at the article. I'd gotten shoved into enough lockers in high school that I was sympathetic toward the Theater Club kids. "It's never fun to get called a fag in front of a room full of people."

"No, I know. I didn't mean to undermine how bad it probably was. Peter used it as an example to show why LGBT kids don't really feel safe so that he could argue that the LGBT dance is one of the few places where these kids can be themselves."

I nodded. It was a fair argument. "I went to the semiformal my first semester. It was nice."

"Did you actually talk to anyone there?"

I shrugged, not appreciating her tone but understanding why she used it. "I spent part of the time talking to this hot senior because he was the only other person there who smoked. I think we spent most of the dance standing outside the Mac, flirting."

Ellie rolled her eyes. "Leave it to you to go to the dance by not going to the dance."

"I did talk to someone, though."

Ellie solved the "how do I fit this giant burrito in my mouth?" problem by neatly cutting hers open and scooping the middle bits up with her fork. I cut mine in half, which didn't really help, and then tried reading Peter's article. I agreed with most of his points, though I was surprised by a paragraph toward the end.

I came out to my parents in high school, he wrote, *and I try to be open when it feels safe to be at WMU, but it still doesn't always feel safe. I imagine there are students all over campus who can't even be themselves in their own rooms because they don't know their roommates enough to confess who they really are. That's a lonely and frustrating way to live.*

Didn't I know it?

"He still hasn't said anything to me one way or the other," I said to Ellie. "I know he's gay because Noel's boyfriend told me, but he never came out to me."

"You haven't come out to him either, have you?"

"I probably should, huh?"

Ellie frowned at her burrito. "I don't know. What is it you want to happen?"

What did I want? I couldn't really imagine a world in which a hot, sunshiny surfer-boy type would ever date a dour, occasionally gothy guy like me, but I sure as hell lusted after him. On the other hand, hadn't Dave said Peter had a thing for gothy twinks? Had he meant me? Was I crazy to let that get my hopes up? Still, all that was kind of beside the point. "I want to apologize for being a dick. I want for us to be friends so things stop being awkward when we're both home. I want to let my guard down when I'm in my own room."

"So maybe coming out will be like a peace offering. Like, you're both gay, so that's something you have in common. You could start by talking about that. Then you can explain that you're just an asshole by nature and you're not being a jerk to him specifically."

"Gee, thanks."

Ellie grinned and shoveled some rice and beans into her mouth. "I love you, Logan. But you *are* an ass sometimes."

"Shut up." Then I grudgingly added, "Point taken."

I TRUDGED back to my dorm after that, rehearsing what I wanted to say. Peter was there when I got back to the room, studying and munching on chips. He greeted me with a little wave and a friendly hello.

Why had I been so mad at him all semester?

Well, I knew why. I liked him. And my anger at my lot in life, all the dread I felt about the preordained future of auditions and performances, needed a place to go. Lord, I really had been an ass.

"Can I talk to you for a minute?" I asked.

Peter closed the book he'd been reading and swiveled on his desk chair to face me. "Sure."

This was so fucking hard. I sat on my bed and took a deep breath. "I wanted to apologize. To you. Because I've said and done some things this semester that were not really fair to you. I've been not super happy with the way this semester has been going, but that's really on me. And I totally misunderstood something you said and got all twisted up about it, but I see now you didn't mean it how I thought you did, so I'm sorry. For being a jerk."

He tilted his head as if I'd just spoken in Swahili. "What did I say that you misinterpreted?"

How to even explain? "Well, see, so, I saw your op-ed in *The Minuteman* today."

He grimaced. "Oh."

"No, I thought it was good. I agreed with it."

He met my gaze. "Okay."

"I'm not… this conversation isn't about the op-ed, I just wanted you to know that I read it. So I know. That you're gay."

He picked up his pen and started twirling it around his fingers. "Okay."

"So, look, I just wanted you to know, I'm gay too, and you said this thing when I gave you a ride to class the other day about a career in theater being gay, and I totally get you were mocking the sentiment, not that you were using 'gay' as a pejorative, but I thought at the time that you were, and… I'm sorry, I really am."

He shifted his weight in his chair and wheeled closer to me. "What are you saying?"

I couldn't look at him, so I stared at the popcorn stucco of our ceiling. "I totally misjudged you, okay? I was wrong to be such a dick. We kind of got off on the wrong foot that night last semester that you yelled at me about smoking, and I let that cloud my judgment."

"Oh, yeah. I forgot about that."

"And then I guess I just assumed you were a straight, dumb jock with no interest in his fey musical roommate, and I was kind of mean to you, and I apologize."

His eyes went wide, but his lips curved into a smile. "You thought I was a dumb jock?"

I took a deep breath and looked at him. He was sitting close to me now, only a couple of inches separating our knees.

"I… yeah. I mean, you *are*, but you're a gay dumb jock, huh?"

He grinned. "I was wondering about what you thought of me, I admit. Not to be stereotypical, because obviously I believe you should be whoever you are, but I guess I thought… but maybe I was projecting?" He shook his head. "You're right, we totally got off on the wrong foot with each other. I guessed you were gay but assumed you were still in the closet."

"Really?" I laughed now, surprised more than amused. "Why did you think so?"

"You never said anything. You don't date."

"Same is true for you, as far as I can tell."

"That's only because I didn't say anything because I thought you maybe had some kind of identity crisis, or you didn't know. Well, I mean, that's not why I didn't date. I did date a little. I went out with this guy Jason for a couple of weeks? Didn't really go anywhere, though. So I didn't mention it to you." He shook his head. "That's not important. I didn't come out to you because I couldn't tell what your deal was, and you're so prickly all the time."

"But you thought I was closeted?"

"I don't know. You're hard to read." He shrugged. "I caught you checking out that guy Ben from the fourth floor when we were doing laundry a few weeks ago, so I was like, 'Oh good, he's not dead inside after all,' but then I thought it was weird that you hadn't said anything. And I was like, 'Hey, I'm pretty easygoing. Logan should be able to be himself around me.' But if *you* thought—"

"Yeah."

He tilted his head. "Well. This may be a rude thing for me to ask, but are you out?"

"Yeah, mostly. I mean, my parents and my friends know. I've dated half the music department." This was a slight exaggeration. I'd dated a bassoonist named Eddie who'd dumped me when he made it into an orchestra in Boston and moved away abruptly, and I occasionally exchanged blow jobs with a hot oboe player named Linus who could do amazing things with his tongue. But this was beside the point.

Peter stared at me for a long moment. "This is very 'Gift of the Magi.'"

"How so?"

"You didn't want to come out to me because you thought I was a dumb jock, and I didn't want to come out to you because I was worried you were in the closet. So basically you sold your hair to buy me a Christmas present while I was out buying you combs for your long, luscious hair."

I let out a confused burst of laughter. "What?"

"It's a strained metaphor, but you know what I mean."

I did. I nodded. "I'm really not as much of an ass as I've been acting all semester. I mean, I probably am a little, but I just thought we had nothing in common."

"We probably don't have much in common besides that we both like boys."

"That can't be true."

He seemed tickled. I was honestly surprised at myself for being so forthright.

"So your op-ed," I said. "When you talked about some gay kids not feeling able to be themselves in their own room, you thought you were talking about me, didn't you?"

"Not just you." He shook his head. "I mean, I thought you were holding yourself back, which means I probably should have talked to you sooner, but I guess I assumed you knew about me because I hang around with the Queer Student Union kids all the time."

"You do?" Didn't he hang out with the football brigade? It took my brain a moment to catch up to the fact that Dave had said he knew Peter through the QSU. "What about Lily?"

"Well, the girl you thought was my girlfriend is actually a lesbian. She's the president of the QSU."

I winced. "There's a 'when you assume…' joke coming, isn't there?"

He shrugged. "You already admitted to being an ass. I accept your apology, by the way."

I didn't know what to say, so I nodded.

"Hey, look at me," said Peter.

I wasn't sure how long I'd been staring at my shoes, but I had to look up to meet Peter's gaze again. Dave's "gothy twink" comment flashed in my mind again as I looked into his eyes. Did he… *like* me? I felt like an idiot for even having the thought, and I assumed he wasn't as attracted to me as I was to him, but hope sprung suddenly, and I leaned forward.

"I'm glad you said something," Peter said.

"I'm sorry," I repeated, though I was caught up in his gaze now. He had really pretty blue eyes. A tuft of his perfect blond hair had fallen out of its coif and dangled over his forehead.

"No, I don't need you to apologize. I accepted it. I understand. I just… that is, since we met, I…." He leaned forward and shook his head. "God, I'm probably about to make this about eighty times worse, but honestly? You being out makes me feel like much less of a perv for finding you attractive."

My heart stopped. "What? Really?"

"Yeah, are you kidding? You've got that dark-haired, pale thing going on." He waved his hand in front of me. I mentally kicked myself for not putting the clues together sooner. "You're so pissed off all the time, but for whatever reason, that just drew me in more. I wanted to… smooth down your ruffled feathers." He shook his head. "Sorry, that sounds stupid."

"No, it's…." It was sweet. Perfect. I was totally charmed, in danger of melting into a puddle right there on my bed. "That's… I mean, you have to know how hot you are." Then I remembered Fred mentioning "that hot guy" in the QSU. "The QSU people I know all refer to you as 'that hot blond guy.'"

He scoffed. "Are you serious?"

"Not to your face, apparently. But yeah. I didn't put that together until just now, but a couple of my friends have been telling me about the hot guy who comes to QSU meetings for months, so he must be you."

"There are other…." He tilted his head. "I mean, it could be Dave or Noel or…."

"*You*, surfer boy. I'm just saying. You're all blond and abs."

He grinned. "You think I'm hot, is what you're saying."

I rolled my eyes, mostly for show. "Don't let it go to your head."

"Well, Logan, if you ever pull that stick out of your ass, I'm right here on the other side of the room."

What was he saying? Did he want me? Was that an invitation? I was too flabbergasted to say anything. He seemed to lose patience, huffing out a breath and leaning away from me. He moved like he was about to stand up, but I couldn't have that, not without figuring out what he really meant.

So I acted. I hooked a hand around his head, pulled him back close to me, and smashed my lips against his.

Peter let out a surprised gasp that feathered over my lips before he kissed me back, opening his mouth like he was trying to devour me. My poor sexually deprived body went instantly on red alert, tingling everywhere as my senses caught up with what my head had decided to do. His lips were soft and his mouth was hot, and he tasted like spearmint gum. The hair at the base of his skull was just as soft as I'd imagined, and his skin was warm and smooth. He put his big meaty hands on my shoulders, and a sigh passed through me. *Finally*, my body seemed to be saying.

He pulled away slightly and met my gaze. "Is this what you want?" he asked softly.

"I've been thinking about it since the first time I saw your stupid, beautiful face."

"I love that you still sound pissed off about it."

Then he kissed me. And I got no studying done that night.

CHAPTER 11

WE DIDN'T have sex that night. I both wanted to and didn't. Just kissing him was totally overwhelming. We made out on my bed for a little while, kissing and copping feels, but everyone kept their clothes on, and at some point in the wee hours of the morning, Peter excused himself. He disappeared for ten minutes and returned wearing pajamas and smelling of toothpaste. He kissed my forehead and went to his own bed.

Having him near me overwhelmed my senses enough that I couldn't think about anything else. Usually on Friday nights, I went down to the FAC to use the practice rooms, because only the diehards practiced on Fridays and it wasn't too crowded. But I'd just spent Friday night making out with a boy instead of practicing.

Once I heard Peter's breathing even out, indicating he'd fallen asleep in his own bed across the room from me, I started to feel guilty. I should have practiced—I'd never get that one section of the Bach concerto we were performing if I didn't, and Costner would be so disappointed….

Except, what the hell? I couldn't take a night off from my rigorous practice schedule to make out with a hot guy? What kind of twenty-year-old was I?

I cursed silently, whispering the word *fuck* over and over like a mantra until my eyelids got droopy.

I did not want this to be my life.

I woke up the next morning with a headache. Peter was gone.

I got up and showered. Took a couple of ibuprofen. Opened my laptop and closed it. Picked up books and put them back down. Sat on my bed. Felt a creeping unease.

What did normal college students do on Saturday mornings? Probably they slept in. Ate brunch. Went shopping in Northampton.

It was too chilly to do anything outside, but maybe I could find something on campus to do, or I could drive into Amherst Center or South Hadley and, I didn't know. Hang out at a coffee shop. See a movie. Waste an hour I never would have wasted otherwise.

Or I could make up for the missed practice.

I wrestled with my decision but ultimately texted Ellie and asked if she wanted to grab waffles at the dining hall before working through the Bach piece together at the FAC. For better or for worse, that was how *I* did Saturdays.

On my way out the door, my mother called. When I answered, she said, "It's loud. Are you outside?"

"I'm on my way to breakfast. Did you need something?" I worked hard to keep the annoyance out of my voice, but I knew I'd failed as soon as my mother made a bristling noise.

"Breakfast so late on a Saturday? That's awfully lazy of you. Aren't you practicing today?"

I was really glad she couldn't see my face. "As a matter of fact, I plan to practice after I eat. But I need to eat, Mom. Or should I give that up too to focus on my violin?"

She gasped. "Logan. How dare you talk to your mother that way."

I pulled the phone away from my face so I could make frustrated noises out of her earshot. Then I put my phone to my ear again. "I'm sorry. I shouldn't have been so mean."

"No, you should not have. I'm only trying to help you. If you don't get in plenty of practice time, you'll never be ready for the December concert. You know how important that concert is."

I did. It was the big game. Orchestra scouts would be there to see me. My veins went icy when I thought about it. I paused outside Ellie's building, trying to regain my composure and also to figure out how to get off the phone with my mother without seeming rude.

"I do take all this very seriously," I said. "I know you don't think I do, but I've been working really hard all semester. Costner picked a challenging program, so I've been doing lots of extra rehearsals."

"All right." She sounded placated. "We put so much time and effort into your violin career. All those lessons, the instruments, the many recitals we attended. Not to mention, you have to keep your grades up to maintain your music scholarship."

"I am, Mom."

"I worry about you, you know."

"I know." Although sometimes I wondered if this worry was more over her own fear of failure and not mine. If I fell flat on my face onstage, how would she react? I had no idea because I'd always been too afraid to let her down—I was too afraid to fail.

"I just called to let you know Ron and Cindy are joining us for Thanksgiving again this year. We'll expect you for dinner."

"Of course."

"I picked up the new bow from the music store for you too. I'll put it in your concert violin case."

"Thanks. I appreciate it. I'll get it at Thanksgiving."

"Good. You work hard, darling. I'll see you in a few weeks."

Ellie walked outside just as I was finally getting my mother off the phone. When she asked what was wrong, I just said, "My mother," and Ellie nodded, understanding as always.

We walked from North Quad to the dining hall together, Ellie buzzing with gossip I didn't care about regarding one of the cello players. I listened, but my thoughts were consumed by Peter. I finally let myself really think about all the questions buzzing through my head.

Why had he just left that morning? Why hadn't he stayed in bed with me? Did he want to have sex with me, or were the kisses just humoring me? Did he want to *date* me? Did I go on dates? Did I want to? Did I have time? Was this going to completely fuck up my housing situation?

"Earth to Logan."

I blinked and looked around. We had to cross a footpath to get to the dining hall, and my brain had apparently shorted out right at the crossing. "What? Sorry."

"Come on, Mr. Head-in-the-Clouds. Waffles are calling."

Fifteen minutes later I had made two big waffles in the iron and put some bacon on top. I was about to dig in when Ellie said, "Did something happen?"

"Huh?" I hated playing dumb with her, but I wasn't ready to talk about Peter yet.

"Did you apologize to your roommate for being such a dick, at least?"

"Oh. Yeah, I did."

"And how did that go?"

"Fine. He took it better than I thought he would."

Ellie peered at me through narrowed eyes. I suspected she was onto me. She waited without speaking. But too much was still undefined and undecided. Given that Peter had just vanished that morning, I wasn't altogether sure I hadn't dreamed the whole thing. I didn't want to tell Ellie about something I didn't know how to process.

So I said, "You have plans tonight?"

Her eyes went wide with surprise. "Yeah. Duh. It's my big date with Tom from the Theater Club."

I'd completely forgotten he'd asked her out. I was a terrible friend. "Oh, yeah. Of course, I'm sorry. Do you know what you're doing yet?"

"Dinner, I think somewhere fancy. Then he wants to go see that improv group that performs at the Mac on Saturdays, and then we might go to a late movie."

"Sounds fun. I didn't know there was an improv group that performs at the Mac."

Ellie looked at me, agog. "They've had a show there every Saturday night since, like, the nineties. They do their auditions each year around the same time the Theater Club does."

I'd had no idea. "Is that what normal college kids do on Saturdays?"

She shrugged. "The group usually gets a big turnout. They're pretty funny. I've seen them a couple of times. That guy Chip from Theater Club is in the improv group too, and he's hilarious."

Did I know a Chip? I couldn't recall his face. "That's good, then. Maybe I'll go sometime."

"I mean, it beats going to one of those big off-campus house parties. I like a party, but last weekend I went with Jane to this party all the way up in Sunderland at this crazy house in the middle of, like, a cornfield, and it was creepy as hell. Everyone was already wasted when we got there. Not exactly my idea of a good time." She shook her head, but then her face brightened. "Oh, I'm supposed to tell you. Noel is throwing a party at his boyfriend's place next weekend. You're totally welcome to come. Peter's probably going too."

"Right. Because his friend Dave is Noel's boyfriend."

She nodded. "You could sound less angry about it. Are you jealous?"

"No." And I genuinely wasn't, not in the way Ellie meant. Because I was completely infatuated with Peter, and he maybe liked me back. "I just feel like a moron for not seeing it and assuming all this time that Peter was straight because he hung out with the jocks. Looking back, there's really nothing I saw that would have led to me making that conclusion besides believing in some stupid stereotypes. But isn't that the kind of thing we've fought against? Like, just because a guy is into classical music doesn't make him gay."

"Lusting after your male roommate is a better indicator."

I sighed. "Shut up."

ELLIE AND I went to practice after brunch, and I stayed an extra forty-five minutes playing sixteenth-note patterns after Ellie ditched me to go get ready for her date. I grabbed a sandwich to go from the Mac on the way back to my dorm, and was surprised to find Peter there when I returned. More accurately, I was surprised to find him half-dressed, sitting on his bed. He seemed to be staring at nothing.

"Going out?" I asked.

"I was going to go out until about three minutes ago."

I put my violin away and waited for him to explain himself. When no answer seemed forthcoming, I asked, "What happened three minutes ago?"

I turned to look at him. He sat on his bed in jeans that were still unbuttoned and a black tank top that he hadn't pulled all the way down yet. His amazing abs were exposed, and the fabric of his shirt clung to his deliciously firm muscles, still damp from a recent shower. He stared unfocused at something near the bottom of my bed.

"Peter?"

He blinked and looked up at me. "Sorry, I… sorry. I was going to go out with Lily. She wanted to check out this bar in Northampton. I was almost ready when she called to cancel. She's not feeling well."

"I'm sorry to hear that."

He met my gaze. "But that's not even… I mean, it's fine. We were going to see a band play, but I hadn't ever heard of them, so it's not a big deal to miss it. Just… my parents called right after Lily did."

"Ah." Now his weird behavior made more sense. Phone calls from my parents always did me in. "Everything okay?"

He let out a breath and leaned forward, resting his forearms on his thighs. "Yeah. They just…. Dad wants me to take an internship during the winter break. I applied for it a little while back, and they called my parents' house to tell them I got it. One month working for this big accounting firm in Boston. The pay is amazing, but I'd have to work fifty hours a week minimum. But it's done. I got it. My father accepted it on my behalf."

"Congratulations?"

He laughed ruefully. "It's like my nightmare."

"I'm sorry your plans fizzled and your parents called. Although at least you had plans. I have a sandwich." I held it up.

He laughed again, genuinely this time. "Wow. I don't want to tell you you're pathetic…."

"No, it's all right. I totally am." I dropped down to sit on my bed. "I am pathetic. I've spent the entire day wondering what normal college kids do on Saturdays because I haven't taken a weekend for myself in forever. Do you know what I did after brunch? I went to the FAC and practiced Bach for two and a half hours."

"Normal is relative," he said. "Do whatever the hell you want to do."

I fell back on my bed, my head near the wall. "That's solid advice. The problem is that I don't know what I want to do. What is there to do on a Saturday night? I always just… practice or study."

It hit me suddenly that Peter and I hadn't really spoken since our little make-out session the night before. My heart began to race as the questions came back. Had I imagined it? Did he not want to mention it? Was it a fluke?

I heard clothes rustling and the floor creak as Peter must have stood up. When I sat back up, he was buttoning up his jeans. That was a shame. That tantalizing glance at the black edge of his underwear had been like a tease, for all four seconds I'd been able to see it. The tank top hid his abs now, sadly, and he shrugged into an eggplant-colored shirt, which unfortunately covered up his arms.

"What are you doing?" I asked. "Are you going out anyway?"

"Get changed. *We're* going out."

"What?"

"You want to know what college kids do on a Saturday night? I'll show you."

"I… okay."

Maybe I was mesmerized by his hotness, but I wanted to break out of my rut, so I did as he said. I pulled a pair of dark jeans and a rarely worn shirt with little glittery pinstripes out of my drawers and quickly ducked into the alcove to change. When I emerged, Peter was messing with his hair in the mirror.

"My hair is being dumb today," he said with chagrin. "Do I look like a mutant, or—"

"You look perfect," I said, because it was true.

He looked me over. "Do you own clothes in colors that aren't black?"

"Not really."

"Then you look perfect too. Let's go."

He grabbed my hand and pulled me out the door.

CHAPTER 12

PETER WAS taking me out, and somehow I still ended up driving. As I watched him fiddle with his seat belt, I remembered that sandwich from the Mac, left out on my desk. The mayonnaise was probably going to spoil while we were out. I spared a thought for the six bucks I'd wasted on it but quickly realized that whatever Peter had planned would probably be better all around.

"Where to?" I asked.

"Let's start at the Pub."

The Pub was a sports bar near campus that served decent food and had become a popular first-date spot for reasons I could not discern. There was nothing even a little romantic about it, at least not that I'd seen the few times I'd been there. But I decided not to derail this date before it got started—if it was even a date; we still had discussed nothing—and just go along with whatever Peter wanted to do, because he clearly had a better grasp on how to have fun than I did.

I found a parking spot in the public lot in downtown Amherst and followed Peter the block or so to the Pub. There was a bouncer stationed at the front who carded us and then refused to give us the hot-pink wristbands we'd need to order alcohol. I didn't care; I wasn't going to drink anyway if I was driving. The hostess brought us to a table near the bar, which I was a little irked by because everyone sitting there was intent on the hockey game playing on the TV and kept reacting loudly to what was happening on-screen.

But I was going to let Peter lead. I was not going to get annoyed.

"WMU is playing tonight," Peter said, glancing toward the TV. "Do you follow the hockey team?"

"I did last year. My roommate was a crazy fan and liked to go to games, so I tagged along sometimes. The WMU team is pretty good."

"Okay. I don't know anything about sports."

"Now that I no longer live inside a shrine to Bobby Orr, I don't pay much attention to hockey anymore. I like football and basketball, mostly."

"Cool." It sounded dumb coming out of my mouth, but I didn't know what else to say. I really did know next to nothing about sports. Bobby Orr could have been a golfer for all I knew, but I guessed from context he was a hockey player.

Peter grinned. He probably sensed my ignorance. "I was on my high school football team."

"Of course you were."

He reached across the table and flicked at the lock of hair that hung in my eyes. "Ah, there's the sarcastic brat I've come to know. You were being so nice to me, I wondered if you'd been abducted and replaced with a pod person."

"I was trying to be nice," I said, probably sounding more defensive than I intended.

"I know. But I want you to be yourself."

When the waitress came by, he ordered cherry sodas for both of us, as well as a bunch of fried appetizers. When she left again, I said, "*You* are really going to eat all that?"

"When I cut loose, I don't half-ass it. Besides, you're going to help me."

I nodded slowly. I tried to come up with a way to broach the topic of kissing and whether now that we'd done a bit of it we were anything more to each other than roommates who found each other mildly annoying. I mentally rehearsed what I wanted to say, but everything I came up with sounded idiotic in my head. After a long minute of silence and mental gymnastics, I temporarily gave up.

Instead I said, "I feel like such a mutant."

"Why do you say things like that about yourself?"

I tried to think of the best way to explain it. "So, okay, in high school, there was this cello player in the orchestra. This girl got straight As and was a cello prodigy, but she didn't otherwise interact with anyone at school. No one made fun of her because she was so insanely talented, but I felt a little sad for her at the time because I didn't see that she had any friends. And when I was in high school, I *did* have friends. Most of them were in orchestra, granted. Actually, my first kiss was on a trip to New York City. A few high school orchestras from around the country had been invited to play at Carnegie Hall as part of this youth festival."

"You've played at Carnegie Hall?"

That was the least important part of this story. I waved my hand. "Yeah, but that's not what I'm trying to say. See, we spent two nights in New York, and the school put us up in this shady hotel that was probably the only reasonably priced place to stay near Carnegie Hall, and I bunked with three other guys. One of them was a flute player named Angelo who I had a crush on. The first night we were in New York, our roommates snuck out to mack on some girls, so Angelo and I got to talking, and then we made out." It was a fond memory. Angelo and I had secretly dated for about five minutes after we got back. He wasn't ready to be out of the closet yet, which I never blamed him for, but the relationship didn't work out, obviously.

"That's a cute story," said Peter, "but what does this have to do with you being a mutant? And we are going to come back to that Carnegie Hall thing, because holy fuck, that's amazing."

I shook my head. I'd gone to an arts high school and had been learning the violin since I was five. Carnegie Hall was impressive, but it felt like just another concert in a lot of ways too. I was proud our orchestra had made it to the festival, but it was a group accomplishment.

I had to close my eyes to think back on what I'd said so far. I never talked this much. I felt like I'd been uncorked. "Anna. The girl from orchestra. I just meant, I made friends with other music kids and made out with a few of them, but she didn't really talk to anyone else. I felt sorry for her, but then somehow in college, I've *become* her."

"You have friends."

I'd *had* friends. I had Ellie now, but we hung out less than we used to; she was only really my friend because we saw each other in rehearsal. I was friendly with some of the Theater Club kids, some of the guys from the Queer Student Union, but those relationships were superficial. And I wasn't really sure Peter counted as a friend either. For most of the semester, we'd barely put up with each other. I didn't think a few kisses had undone that.

Regardless, that was only part of the issue. So I explained, "The worst part is that lately? I've been thinking that I don't really want to be a professional violinist."

Peter jolted upright. "Seriously?"

"Don't get me wrong. I love to play. I love performing. But I think I'd be happier teaching music, maybe playing in a community orchestra or something. There's so much pressure, so much work involved in playing professionally, and I'm already exhausted. The idea of forever auditioning, of jockeying for first chair with other competitive musicians, of traveling all the time? It's not really something I look forward to."

The waitress brought our cherry sodas and a plate of mozzarella sticks and chicken wings.

"This meal will give me a heart attack." I snagged a chicken wing.

Peter suddenly seemed more interested in me than the food. "Why are you a performance major if you want to teach?"

"I thought playing in a famous orchestra was my dream. I pictured myself on a stage in a huge theater hundreds of times. But maybe my parents wanted this for me for so long that I thought it was what I wanted too. I'm not sure anymore."

He nodded. As another waiter brought us a basket of fries, he loaded up his plate. "I know all about parental pressure."

"I know. The accounting thing."

"I've been talking to a professor in the art department about taking a painting class next semester. If you're not an art major, you have to take this survey class first where you do a bunch of shit. Painting, drawing, sculpting, printmaking, whatever. But I showed the professor my work, and she liked it enough that she's going to pull some strings to get me into the intro painting class."

"That's cool. I didn't know you did more than set painting."

"I love to draw. I haven't done much of it lately, but I keep some sketchbooks on my bookcase."

"What do you draw?"

"Oh, anything. People, animals, things I see on campus, sometimes just little doodles and patterns."

"You showed all this to a professor?"

"Yeah. My dad's going to have a fit when he sees that on my schedule, but I kind of don't care anymore. When I started here, I thought I could do it, but my first two years, I mostly took gen ed classes. Now that I have to take a bunch of major classes? I like math, but doing this kind of shit my whole life?"

"Hives."

"Yeah, exactly."

"Changing majors means another year of school for me."

Peter nodded. "I don't know what I'm going to do. Finish, I guess. Take this internship, save some money. Maybe go to grad school for something else entirely." He sighed. "I feel like if my parents are paying, I have to do what they want. But once I graduate and earn some money and can pay my own way? Maybe I study art or design or anything I want."

"Yeah. I can't see you being happy as an accountant."

He tilted his head and gazed at me, looking a little amused. "No?"

"I mean, not that we even know each other that well. But you're so... you. I don't know. Happy and social. I can't picture you crunching numbers and wearing one of those green visors."

He chuckled. "Is that what you think accountants do?"

"I don't know. My parents are friends with theirs. He's this little bald man. Somehow he's married to one of the most flamboyant gay men I have ever met. They used to come over for dinner all the time when I was a kid."

"We had really different childhoods."

Before I was even aware of it, we'd polished off most of the food. I ordered a salad to counteract some of the grease, and Peter ordered a hamburger. He must have had monk-like discipline most of the time to have a body like he did.

"So what are we doing after this?" I asked, still somewhat reluctant to bring up the kissing thing while we were getting along so well.

He flashed me a toothy smile. "I'm glad you asked. Because this is not it right here. We're just fueling up."

I laughed. "I figured."

"We could go see that band in Northampton. Or my buddy Trey is a theater major, and they're doing some kind of one-act workshop thing tonight."

I tried to make my facial expression convey what I thought of *that*.

"So, no. Okay. There are a dozen things. We could go ice skating at the hockey rink. We could see if there are any seats at the basketball game. We could go to the improv show at the Mac. There's an eighteen-plus dance club in Northampton, but it's kind of dead until midnight. We could go see what movies are playing."

I reminded myself that I was letting Peter steer. "I'll go along with whatever you want to do."

His smile turned wicked. "Oh, babe. It's on now."

PETER DECIDED we should drive to Northampton. The band turned out to be a folky female singer-songwriter duo, and they were good, if not really my thing. Despite the mellow tunes, the music was too loud to talk over, and Peter spent a good part of the concert looking at his phone. When the set ended, he said, "Come on," without further explanation.

We walked down the street to a restaurant called Hale's, kind of a middle-of-the-road American place where I'd eaten with my parents a few times. Noel was sitting at the bar. His whole face brightened when he saw us.

"How was the concert?" he asked as he gave Peter a hug.

"Fine. A little boring."

Noel gave me a hug too, which felt awfully forward of him, but I hugged him back. Peter held out a chair for me, so I sat next to Noel at the bar.

"This is Dave's first night bartending solo," Noel explained. "He's been training all semester. I told him I'd keep him company. He was worried he'd scare off the customers. But I'm glad I have other people to talk to now, because he's been so busy I've hardly seen him."

I looked down the bar, and there, indeed, was Dave, pouring a cocktail and chatting with a pair of women. I'd never seen Dave without his baseball cap on before; he had a riot of curly light brown hair.

The restaurant didn't seem that crowded. The hockey game had clearly ended; the TV over the bar was showing *SportsCenter*, and the final score flashed up on the screen. WMU had won, so that was good, I supposed.

"Crowd has thinned since the game ended," Noel said, as if he read my mind.

Dave walked over to us. He seemed tired but happy. "Hi, guys. How's your night going?"

Peter threw his arm around me. "I'm trying to show Logan a wild Saturday night out, but so far I'm failing."

Aw. "I'm having a good time," I said. "Fried food, live music, and now good company. Not the wildest night ever, but it's been fun. You're not failing at anything."

Dave looked between us. Peter still had an arm around me, and I liked it too much to nudge him away. Dave said, "Are you out on a date?"

I honestly had no idea, so I looked at Peter for the answer. He looked back at me, a question in his eyes.

"We could be," Peter said.

I smiled at him. I approved of the idea. It also gave credence to the fact that we had made out in the real world and not my imagination. We'd have to have a bigger conversation about this later, but dating Peter was something I could do. Something I really wanted to do.

It hit me suddenly how insane that was. Dating my roommate was probably a recipe for disaster. What if we broke up and I still had to live with him? Although I'd already proved to myself that I was an expert at avoiding him when I needed to, so maybe that wouldn't be the end of the world. But this was also every bit the porn cliché Ellie kept joking about. Two college roommates hooking up?

Well, all we'd really done so far was make out a little.

Peter frowned. "I can basically see the gears turning behind your eyes. Are you freaking out?"

"No. Just thinking. And not bad things, even. Well, that's a lie. It's basically in my nature to assume that everything is on the brink of disaster. But I wasn't lying when I said I was having a good time."

"Okay." Peter's tone said he wanted to pursue it, but the look he shot at Dave indicated he didn't want to talk it out here.

"You guys are coming to the LGBT semiformal, right?" Dave poured us both sodas. "We need a big turnout or Student Activities is going to kill it."

"I'll be there," Peter said. "You want to be my date, Logan?"

"Depends. Do I have to dress up?"

Peter shot me a wry smile. "I mean, it's a semiformal, so you don't have to rent a tux or anything. A shirt and tie would be fine. You can wear a suit if you want, but a lot of guys probably won't, and it's a QSU event, so I suspect all bets are off."

"Yeah," said Noel. "Nice clothes are encouraged, but there's no real dress code. It's not like we're going to turn you away if you wear a T-shirt."

"I own ties." It came out sounding a little defensive. I had plenty of appropriate clothing, actually, but something about going to a dance filled me with dread. It was about three miles outside of my comfort zone.

"Going to a dance is a perfectly normal thing to do," Peter said, "since you seem preoccupied with being normal."

"I don't really know how to dance."

"That's fine. I'll show you my sick moves." Peter twisted in his seat a little, chair-dancing in a surprisingly sexy way.

I laughed more out of surprise than humor. I put a hand on his shoulder to get him to stop. His eyes sparkled as he gazed back at me.

"Fuck normal," Dave said. "I spent most of my life being 'normal.' Normal is boring."

"What *is* normal, anyway?" Noel asked. "I figure we can all blend in when we're in the real world."

Noel was so ethereally beautiful that I didn't think he'd ever blend in anywhere, but I nodded. "I'm not aiming for that kind of normal. I was telling Peter earlier that I don't know how normal people have fun because I abnormally spend all of my time practicing violin. Music rehearsals ate my semester. That's really why we're out tonight. I'm trying to experience the world like a college student who doesn't live in the FAC would." I shook my head and gestured to my head-to-toe black hair and clothing. "If I were trying to *look* normal, I'm probably failing."

"You *do* look like you walked out of Goth Night at that club down the street." Noel gave me an appraising once-over.

"Plus I'm queer, so I agree," I said. "Fuck normal."

Peter lifted his glass. "Here's to being yourself."

CHAPTER 13

WE HUNG out with Dave and Noel—mostly Noel, since Dave still had to work the bar—until Dave's shift ended around eleven. We parted ways in front of the restaurant, and I led Peter by the hand back to my car.

"That was a pretty typical Saturday night for me," Peter said as we buckled up. "I mean, I'm not the wildest guy. If you'd been hoping for a wild night—"

"The horn section of the orchestra has a house in North Amherst. I've heard their parties are bananas. I could have gone to one of those if I wanted a wild night. You've met me, so you probably know I'm not very wild either."

"You ever been drunk?" Peter asked as I started the car.

"A couple of times. Actually, true story, my first week of school, my roommate dragged me to a frat party, where I got completely wasted and went home with a guy who was trying to pledge the frat. He gave me his number the next morning, but I lost it, and I didn't see him again until a year later when we wound up in a class together."

"Awkward." After a pause, Peter said, "You tell me a lot about guys you've hooked up with."

I *had* brought that up a lot tonight. I hadn't done it on purpose. "Sorry. I think it's the simultaneous subconscious desires to let you know that I'm not a *complete* loser and also that I'm not a virgin."

"Gotcha. I'm not a virgin either."

"Good to know."

Traffic on Route 9 was light, so I pushed the speed limit a bit. Peter fiddled with his phone and then pocketed it and said, "My first time was freshman year. We met at the QSU semiformal, actually. Sweet guy. He graduated last year."

"Did you date him for a while?" My jealousy spiked, and I realized why Peter was probably not thrilled by all my bragging about past conquests.

"A few months. I liked him, but we had different priorities." He sighed. "This is going to make me sound a million years old, but I always pictured myself falling in love in college. You know? Maybe meeting the guy I'd end up with for the long haul. But everyone just wants to hook up."

I was part of that everyone. I hadn't had time for anything more than the occasional hookup. But I could see the appeal of being with someone on a more regular basis. "I don't think you sound old. That sounds nice."

I caught him smiling in my peripheral vision. "Thanks," he said softly.

"I never thought of things that way," I admitted. "Wondering if I'd meet the love of my life in school, I mean. College has been all about my violin. I guess I pictured getting accepted somewhere, the Boston Pops say, and then worrying about romance after that."

"Say you become a music teacher instead. What do you see for your life then?"

I tried to imagine it while keeping my eyes on the road. We still had another ten minutes or so before we'd get to our dorm building. "I don't know. I could see getting a job at a high school around here. Or maybe up north. I like Boston okay, but I'm not really a city person. I think I'd be happy somewhere quieter. Maybe a house in the Berkshires."

"Do you have a husband in this vision?"

"Yeah, I think so. And a dog. Or a few dogs."

"I like dogs," said Peter. I could hear the delight in his voice.

"I never let myself fantasize about this kind of thing. I always focus on one thing. I get a job in a city and live in a shitty apartment and play my violin. The shitty apartment isn't supposed to matter because I'm living my dream."

"But it's not *your* dream."

"And you live in some glamorous penthouse because you're doing absurdly well as a math wizard accountant."

"I'd rather live in the shitty apartment."

"I know." I shook my head. "Fuck normal, huh? Well, fuck expectations too. We're adults. We should have the freedom to choose the life we want for ourselves."

"Easier said than done. If I changed majors, my parents would stop paying for college."

"Yeah, but look at Noel. His parents cut him off, but he's figuring it out." I sighed and turned into the WMU campus. "Ellie says I should wait to change majors. Make sure it's what I really want. I think she's right. I talked to my advisor about possible ways to do what I want. I could finish the BFA and then go to grad school for teaching. I'd have to get a master's to teach anyway." I was considering broaching the subject with my parents too. Maybe I'd tell them that teaching was the backup plan if a major orchestra didn't pick me up. I didn't mention this to Peter, though. The plan still felt too embryonic.

Peter nodded.

"If you could do anything after college, what would it be?" I asked.

"I'm not sure. Something artistic. Theater tech somewhere. Design. I thought for a while about doing technical stuff with movies. My buddy Andy works as a PA for movies being filmed in New York City during the summer. It's grunt work, but he's learning a lot about how movies are made. The behind-the-camera stuff fascinates me. There are engineers for lighting and sound. A lot more goes into operating a camera than you'd think."

"Yeah, I bet."

"I think anything where I got to be creative would be good. Not a lot of creativity in accounting. At least not if you're doing it right. And, I mean, where's the joy in doing people's taxes? Some people probably find that kind of work rewarding, but I don't think it's for me."

"What about the rest of it?" I asked. "Would you get married? Get a dog?"

"Yeah. Definitely. And kids. I'd want to adopt kids."

It was easy to picture Peter as a dad. I didn't see myself as a father type, but I could see Peter being great with kids. He had the kind of enthusiasm for life children were drawn to.

"I don't let myself dwell on that much either," he said quietly. "You're right, I'll probably end up with a great apartment in Boston. I don't know how keen my dad is for me to get married very soon. And probably he still thinks I should marry a woman, have a traditional life. You and I know that will never happen, but I hate how narrow his worldview is."

"Fuck normal," I said. "Fuck traditional."

"Yeah." Peter laughed.

I pulled into the parking lot next to our building. Peter hadn't given up the red parking pass yet, so I fully intended to take advantage of it before the administration caught on and made me surrender it.

We walked silently back to our room. I knew what I wanted to happen here, but I wasn't sure what Peter wanted, and a wave of self-consciousness hit me suddenly. He'd gone to sleep in his own bed the night before. Granted, Peter was a big guy, and both of us squishing into a narrow twin bed was not ideal, but I'd risk getting flattened to sleep beside him. He'd opted not to spend the night with me. He'd said he wanted to date me, but did he want something bigger, something long-term, something physical?

Peter unlocked our door. "This all really has turned on a dime."

"Huh?"

He ushered me inside. After he locked the door, he said, "I just mean, I thought you hated me."

"No. Never. If anything, I hated that I liked you so much. Due to the previously discussed misjudging."

He nodded. "Look, if we could…." Then he shook his head.

I wasn't completely sure how to make a move, and he seemed on the verge of saying something important, so I stood near my bed and waited. When he went about putting his stuff away—including my forgotten sandwich, which he held up and said, "I can toss this, right?"—I decided I should probably just speak up. Holding my tongue had accomplished nothing with Peter.

"Am I misreading things?" I asked.

"What?"

"I mean, you said yourself, this was kind of a date, right? And I've been thinking about what you look like naked for months and we made out a little last night, so I guess I thought tonight we would… but if you don't want to—"

"Why wouldn't I want to?"

I grunted, a little frustrated. "You kind of bailed on me last night. Went back to your own bed. Disappeared in the morning."

He pursed his lips. "I didn't want to rush into anything."

I had no idea what to make of that. I couldn't tell if my own lust was starting to overwhelm my good sense or if he was telling me he didn't want to have sex or what. So I said, "Do you not want me?"

He dropped what he'd been holding—a sock that had gotten free from his meticulously kept dresser—and said, "No, of course I want you. I don't—what are you so mad about?"

Was I mad? I hadn't thought so, but maybe my tone made it sound that way. "Nothing," I said, exasperated. "Why are you cleaning up right now?"

It was his turn to let out a frustrated rumble. He looked down at the sock he'd dropped. Then he looked up at me. "I can never tell what you want from me. And I needed something to do with my hands. I felt awkward, okay? I'm not used to that. I don't normally feel this way. Just around you, I guess."

"I make you feel awkward?"

"I put my foot in my mouth around you all the time. You… I don't know. You kind of muddle me up."

"*I* do?"

"Yeah. It's weird. I was hard half the car ride here, and we weren't even talking about sex. Being near you gets me all hot, and I never feel like I'm quite in control, so I just wanted a moment or two to cool off when we got back, which I can't even get because you're still standing right there."

I riled *him* up? Jesus. "Do you even know the effect you have on me? Do you know how fucking hot you are?"

"Why are we arguing about this?" He was only a tick or two below yelling now.

"I don't know. Why are you cleaning your half of the room when we should be kissing?"

"God."

He was across the room in two steps. He grabbed my face and kissed me hard. And I thought, *Finally.* I put my hands on his shoulders and sank into his body, because finally we were kissing, which was all I'd wanted all night. Well, okay, that wasn't true; I still wanted him naked. I wanted to press our naked bodies together. I wanted to see his cock, feel it, find out what it tasted like.

He deepened the kiss, snaking his tongue into my mouth. I groaned and pressed my hips against his, feeling how hard he already was. That he wanted me this much startled me. But he was in my arms now, kissing me, tasting me, and I gave as good as I got.

He pulled away slightly. "God, you frustrate me."

"Right back at you."

He bit my earlobe. "I want you so fucking much. How could you think I didn't?"

"I can never tell what you're thinking. I think we've amply demonstrated that."

He growled. "Can you now?"

Given that he was nuzzling my neck and had his hands on my butt and his hard cock pressed into my hip, I had a hunch. "Can we be naked now?"

He stilled for a moment. I thought he was angry again, but I realized that he was laughing into my shoulder. He hugged me to him and then pushed me away. I toppled back and landed on my ass on my bed.

"No one has ever made me feel the way you do," he said before whipping his shirt off.

Well, then. I wriggled out of my own shirt as well as I could without unbuttoning it. "Feeling's mutual."

He unbuttoned his jeans and pushed them down his hips. His hard cock was clearly outlined in his little black briefs. I thanked whichever god of engineering had invented those things, because they offered me this magical, tantalizing glimpse of what Peter was packing, and his big body, with all those muscles, was a perfect frame.

"You are so sexy," I said before bowing forward and pressing a kiss to his belly button.

"I want to fuck you so bad," he said.

That seemed like a lot for a first date. "Um, about that."

"Are you a top?"

"No, but… I mean, I want to, but not tonight. Let's work up to that. Okay?"

He nodded and climbed onto the bed with me. "Whatever you want to do. Take off your pants."

I giggled nervously. It was hard to be around him sometimes. His skin was less tan now than it had been at the beginning of the semester, but he was still blond and beautiful, and I was so pale and skinny, and I felt unworthy. "Peter, I—"

His face softened. "What is it?"

I'd gotten nervous suddenly, but I didn't know how to tell him that. I blurted, "Do you really have a thing for gothy twinks?"

He titled his head. "Who told you that?"

"Dave."

"Dave has a big mouth. I don't know what I have a thing for, except you. I have this for you." He cupped his cock. God, that was hot. "Will you relax?"

That he'd finally read me right was something of a revelation. It put me at ease. "Yeah, okay." I slid off my pants. My underwear was far less interesting than his, just simple blue cotton boxers, which was maybe why he pulled them off immediately.

Or he wanted me to be naked. Which I now was.

He pressed his face against the space where my thigh met my hip and inhaled deeply before nibbling at the skin. When his mouth circled the tip of my cock, I threw my head back, unable to cope with what was happening. Peter—smoking hot, unavailable Peter—licked and sucked on my dick. He overwhelmed me, made my skin come to life, made me question reality. I ran my hand over his soft hair, in awe of him. He moaned around me like he was just as worshipful of me as I was of him. Somehow this was my life.

"Fuck," I grunted, thrusting up into his mouth. His goddamn perfect mouth.

I didn't want to come too fast, so I pushed at his shoulders. "Turnabout is fair play."

He looked at me quizzically.

"I love your little briefs, but I need you to take them off now."

Without even moving much, he managed to get his briefs off while remaining on all fours in front of me on my bed. His cock was huge and perfect, just like the rest of him; it was hard and pointed up toward his belly. After he tossed the briefs aside, I grabbed his head and kissed him. He slunk forward and sank on top of me. I opened my legs for him to fit between, and he lined his cock up with mine. I groaned under his touch, aroused and relieved that we were finally together like this. I thrust against him to show what I wanted, and he thrust back, taking both of our cocks in his hand and stroking them together. We both moaned.

Being with him was… too much.

"I'll come fast," I said breathlessly.

"That's okay. It's not like this is our one shot."

One dumb sentence and I knew that meant he wanted us to be together again, probably into the foreseeable future. I put my arms round him and pulled him close again. I didn't know—I doubted, actually—that we'd be together any longer than the current semester, which was quickly winding down, but I wanted him for as long as he'd have me, and in this moment, with me riding the edge of an orgasm, it felt like he was mine.

So I let go. I surrendered to him. I thrust against his hand, his cock, his hip, searching for purchase, wanting to get *there*, my body screaming that if I thrust just once, twice more, the world was full of promise.

And then he groaned and came first.

He scrunched up his nose and eyes as if he were concentrating deeply on something, and then everything went slack as he moaned and cursed and spilled on my cock, on my belly, and my body couldn't help but follow. He nuzzled my neck again and I came, sighing and crying out and pumping against him.

As I came down, he kissed me, nibbled on my lower lip. I held him tight, ran my hands over his shoulders, felt the full breadth of him. He amazed me. And he wanted me. How was this my life?

When he pulled away, I looked up at him. He was smiling.

"Do you believe that I want you now?" he asked.

"I believe you."

He pressed the whole weight of himself on me. He rested his head on my pillow for a second, and then he practically hopped out of bed. I was starting to feel drowsy, but he was apparently one of those guys who wanted to run laps after sex. But instead of putting clothes on, which I expected, he pulled a packet of wet wipes out of his desk drawer. He came back over and wiped off my abdomen.

"I know this isn't romantic, but I was feeling sticky," he said as he wiped himself off too. He held up the used wet wipes. "You'd be surprised how often these come in handy, especially since there's no sink in here."

"I don't really need to know when they've been useful before, but okay."

"It's possible I jerk off to porn while thinking about you when you're at orchestra rehearsal."

Good Lord.

"You should see your face right now," he said, giggling softly.

"Next time you do that, promise to record a video?"

He laughed harder and tossed out the wet wipes. Then he returned to my bed. I scooted as far over to the side as I could, and he curled around me. He was still naked. Peter should always be naked, as far as I was concerned.

"You surprise me," he said.

"How so?"

"I thought you had a stick up your ass, and you *are* wound pretty tight, but you have a dark side waiting to be let loose."

"I do?"

"Yeah. You've got something wild in you. I like that."

"Okay. If you say so."

He hugged me close. I leaned into his warm skin. He said, "We'll rebel together, here in this room, even if no one else knows about it."

I understood the contradiction in what he was saying, but I knew what he meant too. It wasn't about sex; it was about being who we wanted to be, away from the expectations of others. "Yeah." I rested my head on his arm and looked up, meeting his gaze. "Yes."

CHAPTER 14

I TOOK what Peter and Noel said about being normal to heart and decided, basically, *fuck it*. When I went to get my hair cut the following week, I walked into the salon and said, "Let's do something different."

I'd had the same dumb haircut, more or less, since high school. It was fairly traditional: short in the back, a little longer on top, the bits hanging over my forehead the only nod to style.

I usually got my hair cut at a salon in Amherst by one of the younger stylists who was technically still training, but when you got the same haircut that more than half the men in America got, it was not a great challenge to the stylist. When I told her I wanted her to get creative, she seemed to relish the opportunity. When the clippers came out, I almost bolted, but I let her do what she would. I walked out of the salon with the sides of my head shaved, super short hair in the back, and long spiky locks that fell over my eyes.

I loved it.

I drove back to the dorms because I needed to grab my violin before my evening rehearsal. I must have caught Peter right before his postgym shower, because he was wearing only warm-up pants and was furiously wiping his face with a towel. Thus he didn't see me when I came in, and merely grunted a hey.

"Hey. I got a haircut."

"Oh yeah?" Peter picked his head up and looked at me. "Whoa. That's... hot."

"Yeah?"

"Yeah. I really like it. Can I touch your head?"

Considering some other places his hands had been, I was surprised he felt the need to ask. "Yeah. Of course."

He walked over and cupped his hand around the side of my head. He rubbed gently and wrinkled his nose. "Softer than I would have expected. Definitely a sexy haircut, though."

"You like it?"

"Yes." He leaned over and dropped a quick kiss on my lips. "You look amazing. With your dark hair, it's kind of gothy and dangerous."

I grabbed him by the shoulders and pulled him close so I could kiss him properly.

He stepped away gently. "I'm fresh from the gym. I must smell pretty ripe."

"I like it."

"Sure. You would. But I really want a shower, and I know you have rehearsal." He held up a finger. "But I was thinking. I still owe you dinner."

"Huh?"

He rubbed the side of my head again. "I promised you dinner in exchange for chauffeuring me around campus when I was injured. And since you're kind of my boyfriend now, I thought maybe we could go somewhere a little fancy."

"You think I'm your boyfriend."

He frowned. "Are you not?"

I hadn't really given it a lot of thought prior to that moment, but I liked the idea of him being my boyfriend. I smiled. "I am."

He smiled back. "Good."

"But we already went to dinner that one time."

"We're not limited to one date, Logan. Look, Dave is hooking me up with the employee discount for that fancy Italian place in Northampton. I want to pay you back both for driving Miss Daisy—" He paused and gestured toward himself. "—and for, you know, all the good loving this week."

I laughed despite myself. "All right."

"The LGBT semiformal is next week too, so here's what I was thinking. Maybe before the semiformal, we get all dolled up, go have a nice dinner, and then come back to campus to dance our asses off. Get a little bump and grind going on the dance floor." He demonstrated, stepping away from me and showing off a few of his moves. He even twerked, which surprised me so much I giggled. God, he was sexy, even when he was dancing while making goofy faces. "What do you say?"

I'd hooked up with a few guys in my time at WMU, but I'd never had a real boyfriend. I hadn't known how much I wanted one until I started making out with Peter regularly. "That sounds good."

He grinned. "Good. It's a date." He moved back over and kissed me. I rubbed his shoulders. Then he pulled away again. "I don't want to make you late. I'll tell you more about how sexy I find your haircut tonight."

I understood that to mean "we'll be making out a lot later," so I gave him a peck on the cheek and grabbed my violin.

In order to clear my head, I decided to walk to rehearsal instead of driving. Most of the time, I drove because it was convenient to do so, but the FAC was only a fifteen-minute walk from my dorm, and sometimes driving took longer because traffic on campus was always impossible at this time of day. The WMU campus sprawled out across several square miles, and the walking paths were more navigable than the streets. I was particularly skilled at getting stuck on the narrow campus roads behind the campus shuttle bus, which made approximately 1,324 stops as it looped around the classroom buildings in the middle of campus. The trip down the hill on foot from North Quad to the FAC was an easy walk, I just liked my car.

When I got to rehearsal, Ellie was sitting in her chair, and I realized I hadn't told her Peter and I were dating now. I'd been in this happy bubble of sexually satisfied bliss for a few days, but nobody knew about it. I couldn't have said why I hesitated to tell Ellie, but I was reluctant to speak up. Would that make this any less real?

On the other hand, I wanted to know how her date had gone. And it wasn't like I needed a pretense to speak with her.

But as I unpacked for the rehearsal, she walked over. "I love what you've done to your hair. It's so funky."

"Thanks." My face heated up at the compliment and the memory of Peter feeling up my head.

"What prompted the change?"

Fuck normal, I thought, but I said, "I don't know. I wanted something different." I looked around. The orchestra was still filtering in. "How was your date this weekend?"

"Amazing! I'll tell you all about it after rehearsal."

Costner came in and banged his baton on his music stand a bunch of times before we got into it. He spent a good chunk of rehearsal yelling at the violas and cellos for not getting the rhythm quite right on the Bach concerto. He made me play my solo about six hundred times too, which was fine; we'd been working on it in class and I felt confident in it.

Playing my violin was sometimes an out-of-body experience. I'd practiced this solo so much, muscle memory commanded it. Sometimes I listened to what I was doing and critiqued myself: that note was a little flat, that run of sixteenth notes is too slow, the syncopation is off a little. Sometimes I drifted away and thought of something completely unrelated to music. Sometimes I was conscious of the fact that the entire orchestra and Costner were watching me play and I got so self-conscious, I overthought what I was doing and made mistakes.

At the end of rehearsal, we did one last run-through of two of the concert pieces. Costner made me stand beside him, stage left, as if we were doing the concert just then. He was testing whether I'd memorized the solo by making me stand away from the music, but I still felt mildly silly standing while the rest of the orchestra played behind me. Luckily I knew it like a nine-year-old violinist knows "Hot Cross Buns" or anyone who has ever taken piano lessons knows "Chopsticks." I didn't relish being in the spotlight; I would rather have sat with the orchestra. But as concertmaster, I was the star.

When rehearsal ended, Ellie approached as I packed up my violin. "That was intense."

I nodded. "I walked here. You want to walk back with me? I want to hear about your date, and I have to tell you something."

Her eyes danced. I suspected she already knew what I wanted to tell her.

We were about ten paces past the door of the FAC when Ellie said, "So tell me."

I took a deep breath. "That whole apologizing-to-Peter thing seems to have worked out."

She squealed. "I knew it! You're totally in love now, aren't you?"

"What? No. We've made out a lot, and I agreed to be his date to the LGBT semiformal next week. We're not getting married or anything."

She punched my arm lightly. "That's perfect. I'm so happy for you."

I wanted to protest. I couldn't have said why, but so much unbridled positivity made me want to lash out, but instead I giggled—giggled, geez—and smiled.

"How are things going with Tom? The date went well, clearly." I wanted to deflect attention from my reddening face.

"Good! We're going out again Friday. He's a total sweetheart and he's really fun to hang around with. He tells the best jokes. Kind of a dry sense of humor. We went to that Italian place in Northampton for dinner, and we sat talking for, like, three hours. I think the waitstaff hates us for taking up a table for so long, but it was very romantic."

"I'm glad that's working out. I'm really happy for you."

"I haven't gotten naked with him yet, but maybe soon. North Quad is doing that dance in December. Maybe I'll see if he wants to go to that. What do you think?"

"I think that sounds nice." Well, a North Quad dance sounded like a nightmare to me, but it was the sort of thing Ellie got excited about, so I didn't want to rain on her parade.

"Look at us losers finally finding romance."

"You're not a loser. You're great, Ellie. You're smart and sweet and pretty, and Tom is lucky to have you."

She shifted her shoulders in an "aw, shucks" gesture. "Thanks. But you said I'm not a loser. Do you think you're a loser?"

"Up for debate. Peter seems to like me anyway."

"That's all that matters, I guess."

CHAPTER 15

THANKSGIVING FELT a little like a jail sentence.

I'd been avoiding my parents. I let their calls go to voice mail more often than I picked up, and when I did talk to them, I tried to get off the phone as fast as possible. I was still working out what I wanted to do after I graduated, I wasn't ready to tell them about Peter yet, and I didn't want to deal with the continuing pressure to be a brilliant concert violinist.

I hadn't even planned to spend the entire long weekend in Springfield. I figured I'd eat dinner with my parents on Thursday, maybe spend the night, and then get back to the WMU campus as fast as possible. Peter had a similar plan. He'd caught the bus to Boston Wednesday night to see his own family in Brookline, just outside Boston, and he'd said he would come back Friday night, on the pretense of needing the quiet away from his family to get some big assignment done. In reality he didn't want to deal with his father, who had called him almost daily the week before to talk about the big internship in Boston. I could see how unhappy Peter was whenever he and his father spoke, and it bothered me, but I couldn't think of how to help besides just to listen when he complained afterward.

A couple of weeks after we'd first kissed, things with Peter were going well. We had talked about putting our beds side by side, but as soon as we started moving the dorm furniture around, it became a bigger project than either of us wanted to embark on, so we'd settled for trading off whose bed we slept in. Sharing a twin bed with Peter was not doing great things for my back, but I didn't care. I figured if we were still together next semester, we could worry about the furniture configuration then.

I drove home to Springfield Thanksgiving morning. Aside from seeing my parents, I also planned to get my gray suit out of my closet—the semiformal was a week away—and grab my concert violin. I dreaded dinner, which was to be a formal affair with my parents and friends of theirs, a couple who owned a theater in the Berkshires that was a popular stop for a lot of touring casts of Broadway productions. I found them insufferable; they loved to talk at length about *The Theater* as if they were putting on Shakespeare and not second-run performances of *Wicked*. Not that I didn't love *Wicked*, just that I recognized it was not the sort of production literary scholars would be writing about in a hundred years.

I debated how much to tell my parents about what was going on in my life. I was curious to see if they, my mother in particular, would react to the fact that I had a boyfriend. I was tempted to bring up the music education plan too, but that was a lot for a visit I didn't intend to last more than twenty-four hours. Springfield was only a thirty-five-minute drive from WMU, and I wanted to be in bed with Peter Friday night.

With Peter still on the brain, I pulled into the driveway of my childhood home. Then the bubble burst. The first thing my mother said to me after I walked through the front door was "What on earth did you do to your hair?"

My dad was out picking up Ron and Cindy, presumably so he could drive them home later after Cindy had too many glasses of wine. My mother insisted I sit down in the kitchen to talk to her while she finished making dinner.

I watched her baste the turkey and peek in several of the pots on the stove. "I'm making homemade cranberry sauce this year," she said. "I got the recipe from a woman at work. Just thought I'd try something new instead of eating the stuff from the can."

"Aw. I kind of like the stuff from the can."

"I know, darling, but this will be better. Now tell me what's going on with you. We've hardly talked at all lately. How's school?"

"Good. Classes are hard, but I should get As in most of them. Costner has been pushing me hard, but, you know, the December concert is a big deal."

"Will there be orchestra directors in the audience?"

My mother knew well that Costner treated the December concert like the orchestral equivalent of an important football game. He invited all of the orchestra directors he knew to come scout his best musicians. "He said so. I have three solos, so they'll see plenty of me."

"That's excellent, sweetheart."

I walked over to the counter and snagged a dinner roll, which Mom tried to slap out of my hand. I danced away from her and shoved the whole thing in my mouth. It was buttery and delicious. Mom rarely cooked, even though she was good at it, so Thanksgiving was always the rare culinary bonanza in our house.

I waited to see if there would be follow-up questions. When there weren't, I said, "Also, I, um, started dating a guy."

There was a long pause. "Really?"

"Yeah. His name is Peter." I did *not* add that he was my roommate. Mom rarely seemed interested in anything that wasn't related to my violin, so I didn't think I'd ever mentioned my roommate's name to her, or if I had, she probably didn't remember it. If she asked, I'd confess, but the last thing I wanted was for her to picture all the alone time we spent together. Instead I said, "He's an accounting major. Does a lot of stuff with the Theater Club. They're putting on *Oklahoma!* this semester. I decided not to do pit because Costner put me in extra rehearsals."

"That's good. Better for you to focus on what matters and not on extracurricular shows. And I don't know about dating this boy."

"He's a great guy, Mom."

"I'm sure he is, but I don't want you to do anything that will take away from your music studies."

Ah. Of course. Nothing to jeopardize my future.

"It's not that serious." I felt like I was betraying Peter as I spoke. "We're just seeing each other. I thought you'd be happy that I'm not completely lacking in social skills."

"Oh, of course, darling. I want you to be happy. I'm glad there are people at school who you connect with. I just know that sometimes relationships can be a distraction."

"I won't let this be. I haven't missed a single rehearsal all semester, and I basically have a practice room at the FAC with my name engraved on the door, I'm there so much. And Peter studies more than I do, so he's not a distraction. I really like him, Mom."

She turned toward me, away from the burbling pots, and pursed her lips, giving me her sour disapproval face.

Since I'd already earned her ire, I decided to keep pushing. I wanted to at least drop the hint and see what her reaction would be. "Also, I was thinking. What if no orchestras accept me?"

My mother gasped. "You're a brilliant musician, Logan. That won't happen."

"But just in case. What do you think of me going to grad school for music education? I think I'd like teaching."

"You've worked toward violin performance your whole life. You want all those hours you spent practicing, all that money we spent on lessons, to go to waste?"

"I'd still play. Just on a lesser scale. And I'd take what I learned in those lessons and apply it to teaching."

But my mother shook her head. "Is this boyfriend of yours putting ideas in your head?"

"What? No. It's something I've been thinking about for a while. I need a backup plan. Orchestras are really competitive. In the event I don't get chosen for one some year, I'd like to have another career to fall back on. I'd still be doing something music related."

"Nonsense. Keep working hard and you'll get it. You're enormously talented. It would be a shame to waste all that talent on *teaching*." She said "teaching" as if I wanted to work in a brothel. The message was clear: as far as my mother was concerned, teaching was beneath me.

"All right. It was just an idea." I watched her silently for a few more minutes, feeling defeated. But at least I had one positive thing to look forward to. "While I'm here, I want to get my gray suit. Do you know where it is?"

My mother nodded. "It's in your closet upstairs. I had it dry-cleaned after the last time you wore it. Why do you need it?"

"I'm going with Peter to a semiformal dance next week."

"On a weeknight? Shouldn't you be focusing on rehearsals?"

Anger bubbled up in my chest. That was new; I was so used to acquiescing to my parents' wishes that this resistance was unfamiliar. But I liked it. It burned in me, reminded me that what I wanted was something else from what they wanted. Today was probably not the day to begin my protest, though. "The dance is after practice Thursday." This was a lie. I'd actually already talked to Costner about taking a night off. Costner had seemed enthusiastic, wanting me to enjoy myself at the dance. I suspected he realized he'd been monopolizing my time. He probably would have been less willing to part with me if I hadn't mastered all three of my solos. I was concert-ready. One night off wouldn't derail my performance.

"All right. Well, do what you want. As long as it doesn't interfere with school."

"No, I know." I sighed. "I do really like this guy, Mom. I don't know if it will work out. But my life can't be all music all the time. I'll go crazy."

She frowned. "You can focus on other things after you get into a good orchestra."

"Yeah." I took a deep breath, trying to keep my frustration at bay. "I'm gonna go look for the suit, okay?" I got up from the table and went up to my room.

"Your father will be back soon. Don't spend too long upstairs."

I seethed the whole time I sorted through my closet. I probably yanked on my old clothes harder than I needed to, and found my suit still wrapped in plastic from the dry cleaner. How dare Mom imply I shouldn't date Peter. My parents had met in college. Mom had been an aspiring flautist who had never been good enough to do more than play in her college's orchestra, and Dad had been a voice major who stopped singing after he graduated to focus on his real job at a bank. Now they channeled all of their creative energies into me, as if I could be the child who lived their dreams. I had no siblings, so I was the singular focus of their devotion, and it exhausted me. Part of me wished I'd gone to school farther away; I never quite felt like I was free from under their thumb.

But maybe it wouldn't have mattered. Even at school I felt tremendously guilty for wanting something beyond the path they'd laid out for me.

I took the suit out of the closet. I hung it on the closet door so I'd remember to grab it when I left. I'd always liked this suit; it was well-tailored and fit me well. My parents had bought it for me the year before, when we'd all gone to a very formal wedding. I had a dark red tie that I thought would go with it nicely. I looked over the suit, imagining myself wearing it with Peter by my side. I liked that image of us, all dressed up, out for a romantic night.

I had just located the tie when I heard Dad's car in the driveway. Cindy's upper-class accent rang through the air, and the car doors slammed.

I jogged back downstairs, where Mom waited near the front door. "Are you upset?" she asked quietly.

"No."

"You seem upset."

"I'm fine, Mom." I walked over to the living room piano, the one my parents bought when I was five, the one my private tutors had used to tune or accompany me during lessons. I could play the piano some. Not as well as the violin, but I'd had to learn as part of my overall music training. Plunking out a melody on a piano could sometimes help me understand what a piece of music was supposed to sound like.

"You can tell me if you're upset. Before Ron and Cindy come inside."

I took a deep breath. "Just… try not to pin all your hopes and dreams on me getting into an orchestra. You know I'd move to

Boston tomorrow if the Boston Pops wanted me. I just think it's a long shot. I'm the best violinist at WMU, but I'm competing with kids who went to actual music schools like Berklee and Juilliard. I wasn't good enough for those schools, remember?" She certainly reminded me often enough.

"You've gotten so much better since you started at WMU. Professor Costner is an excellent teacher."

"He is, that's very true." I let out a breath and ran my fingers over the top of the piano. "We'll see, okay?"

Dinner was… slow. Mostly I ate and listened. Cindy and Ron regaled us with tales of their vacation to Vietnam, and then Cindy delivered a monologue about the importance of theater in a community. I nodded my way through a conversation about the importance of arts education. It wasn't that I disagreed, it was just that everyone at the table was so pretentious. It only got worse the more wine Cindy and Ron consumed. I was grateful when Cindy started slurring her words and Dad announced it was time to drive them home.

While they were gone, I went into the study to look at my concert violin. Mom followed me in there.

The violin was among my most prized possessions, an antique I only used in performances, and I needed it for the upcoming December concert. I opened the case to make sure everything was as it should be. My mother hovered, which annoyed me, but I ignored her as I checked the contents of the case. It had two bows in it, one of which was broken—the nut I turned to adjust the tension of the hair was stuck and wouldn't move more than a quarter turn anymore—and should have been tossed, but I'd hung on to it as an emergency backup. The other bow was brand-new, one my mother had purchased for me after I'd complained that the one I used every day probably needed to be replaced. A round puck of rosin wrapped in a handkerchief rested in one of the pockets. I picked up the violin itself. It was made of a piece of maple with orange undertones. The varnish shone in the waning sunlight coming through the study window. Everything was in order, though the bridge was starting to warp. I had a couple of replacement bridges back in my dorm room, though, so I could fix that when I got back to school.

The truth was, I'd fallen in love with the concert violin the first time I saw it at a music store during a trip to New York City when I was fifteen. I'd been eyeing it as we window-shopped, and the clerk asked if I wanted to play it. As soon as the bow stroked against the string to make that first note, I'd wanted it. The sound was so much richer than my practice violin. That was how it worked with violins; often the older the better. Newer models didn't generally resonate the same way. The wood on this one in the store in New York was weathered. It was clear it had been refinished a number of times. The pegs were a different kind of wood than I'd ever seen before, kind of a marbled brown, not the usual black pegs that seemed common in student violins. I'd stood in the middle of that store and played what I could remember from the Bach partita I'd been learning as an audition piece. That violin was made for me.

The clerk immediately went about negotiating with my parents. It hadn't been cheap.

My mother stared at me expectantly, so I picked up the new bow. I played the first thing that popped into my head, a Bach minuet every violin student had to learn at some point in their training. It came out a little scratchy—the new bow had no rosin on it, my chin rest was back at school, and the violin hadn't been tuned in months—but my mother seemed pleased.

I put the violin back and closed the case again. I pressed a hand to the top of it. I did love this instrument. I loved to play it. I planned to play it well into old age.

"It looks good?" she said.

"Yeah, it looks great. Thanks for keeping it." I didn't really have room for it in my dorm room, and the temperature control in the dorms was spotty at best, so I didn't like storing it at school.

"You need anything? You're good with school supplies? Rosin? Extra strings?"

"I'm fine, Mom. I really just needed the suit and the concert violin. I'll take those up to school tomorrow."

"I wish you'd stay a few more days."

"I know. Thank you for dinner. You outdid yourself this year."

She hugged me and kissed my cheek. "I love you, Logan. You know that, right? Your father does too. We want to make all your dreams come true."

"I know." But the line between my dreams and theirs had seemed less blurry lately. Resentment and fatigue simmered in my belly, but with no real place to put them, I didn't know what to say or do. So I added, "Thanks."

"Of course. Now, can I talk you into a piece of pie? We won't tell your father."

She seemed practically giddy as she led me back to the kitchen and took a beautiful—although store-bought—apple pie out of the fridge. As she cut us each a slice and put a healthy dollop of whipped cream on top, I thought about all that had happened that day. I did know my parents loved me. They had been incredibly supportive of my musical ambitions for my entire life. As we ate pie together, I tried to push my resentment aside and enjoy our time together.

"Thanks, Mom," I said.

Her expression seemed knowing, like maybe she knew exactly what I was thanking her for. "Of course, sweetheart. Now eat up before your father gets home. This will be our little secret."

CHAPTER 16

PETER REALLY did go all out for the semiformal. He bought us both boutonnieres and grinned the whole time he pinned mine on my lapel. It was adorable. Then we had dinner at a fancy Italian restaurant in Northampton, where I had to concentrate very hard on not getting marinara on my suit. He kept up a steady stream of babble throughout our meal, mostly about how annoying he found his classes and about how he was thinking about joining the intramural football team in the spring and on and on.

On the drive back to campus, he said, "You've been quiet."

"Sorry. Lot on my mind."

"Want to talk about it?"

I recognized that one of the things that worked with me and Peter is that we clicked when I was straightforward and honest. I felt like I could tell him anything and I'd get no judgment. So I said, "This is the first night off from rehearsal I've taken all semester, aside from the holiday, and I know I deserve a night off, and I'm happy to be spending tonight with you, but I feel a little guilty."

"Don't."

"I know I shouldn't. I *know*. But I keep hearing my mother's voice in my head."

Peter reached over and took my hand, which had been fiddling with a loose slip of paper in one of the cup holders between the two front seats.

"I will do my best to make you forget your guilt tonight, how's that?" he said.

I nodded without taking my eyes off the road. I'd need my hand back to deal with a tricky turn when we got back to campus, but I laced my fingers with his and squeezed, unwilling to give up his touch until the last possible moment. I knew he understood exactly what I was feeling, that he had a lot of the same worries about the future as I did. I appreciated his company a great deal for that reason. We got each other. That was important.

Dinner had gone longer than anticipated. I wasn't upset about that; I didn't know very many of the people who'd be at this dance, and I dreaded it somewhat. What did one do at a dance? Would I be expected to talk to people? Would I have to display my nonexistent dance skills?

When we arrived back at the Mac, the dance was already in full swing. The music was loud, which I was not such a fan of at first. Peter and I had both opted for pretty traditional suits, but "semiformal" was obviously more a guideline than a rule fashion-wise tonight. Fred danced wildly with a guy I didn't know; Fred wore suspenders and a glittery bow tie paired with a very tight pair of red pants. Noel wore an insane plaid suit. Dave kind of looked like his mother had dressed him, in a white shirt and black pants, neither of which quite fit. Lily appeared to be wearing a replica of Molly Ringwald's dress from *Pretty in Pink*. Generally it was a garish display of bright colors and, in a few cases, seminudity. Like if a Pride parade went to prom.

Rainbow streamers and lots of glittery baubles hung from anything that would support them—little disco balls, bits of iridescent tinsel, sparkly gewgaws. Each table had what looked like a homemade centerpiece, and these varied—a few tables had tiny piñatas or flowers made out of tissue paper, that kind of thing. I felt like I could see the handiwork of a few of the craftier Theater Club kids here. I thought it was gaudy, but the decorations had a certain vibrant appeal to them. The space felt tacky and welcoming.

Peter took my hand and led me into the room. We greeted Noel and Dave and a few of Peter's other friends. They were gathered around one of the tables—this one had a papier-mâché centerpiece shaped like a cowboy hat with a rainbow ribbon tied around the brim—and Noel was talking excitedly about something, but I wasn't really listening. I thought about the editorial Peter had written for *The Minuteman* and recalled that he thought this dance was important because it was a safe space for the LGBT students. Including me. It was strange, because I hadn't really ever felt a part of anything except an orchestra, but the people here kept saying, "Hi, Logan," in a friendly way. Peter introduced me to his friends and kept touching me as he did it, clearly signaling we were together. This was my community. Dave and Noel were becoming my friends too. It overwhelmed me now to actually feel like I belonged. I mentally made fun of the Queer Student Union kids a lot, but it was hard to deny that they'd done a good thing here.

I enjoyed the thrum of the music in my chest, despite its loud volume, as I chatted with people who were becoming my friends. I was charmed by Peter's enthusiasm for all of it. My discomfort with the situation melted away and I was enjoying myself. Then Peter asked me to dance.

"I don't really dance," I said.

"It doesn't matter. You don't have to be good at it. You just have to move."

Peter moved his big body around with a deftness and agility I could never hope to possess, but I could only throw my arms around awkwardly, my unsure feet suddenly stuck to the floor. We did manage to work up a sweat, so I went to get a drink and find a place to stash my jacket while Peter continued dancing. He looked effervescent as he did so, and I watched him get down as I waited in the line for the bar. Several people—guys, girls, it didn't seem to matter—came over to dance with him, and he let everyone rub against him, which got my hackles up, even though I knew it was all in good fun. But it highlighted for me that everyone loved Peter. I felt like a black rain cloud.

The bartender gave me a bottle of water, which I downed in one gulp. I asked for another and walked over to the table where Noel was holding court.

"You look like you feel as awkward as I do," said Dave.

"I came to one of these freshman year but spent most of the night outside smoking, so I guess that doesn't count. I'm not really sure what to do."

Dave shrugged. "You dance. You hang out. If you're me, you take comfort in the fact that a man almost everyone here wants will be going home with you later."

"I know how that is." Fred hit on Peter in the middle of the dance floor, and I wanted to kill him.

"The whole point of this thing is to make it so that you don't feel shame at being with who you want to be with."

"I don't feel shame."

Dave smiled ruefully. "I wish I could say the same. Not that I feel shame at being with Noel, but it took me a long time to accept this part of myself, you know? The queer part, I mean. I catch myself falling into old thought patterns. Looking over my shoulder a lot. You know?"

I nodded, but my issues were so much bigger than whether I was gay. Maybe I'd feel differently about that if I went somewhere other than a big university in a blue state, but I felt pretty safe on campus. And my parents clearly cared more about whether a love interest was distracting from music than what his gender was.

Fred was grinding on Peter now.

"If you'll excuse me, I need to go peel one of my friends off my boyfriend," I said.

Dave patted my back.

Fred saw me as I approached. He winked. There was a lull in the music, so it was quiet enough for him to say, "Logan, there you are. You've been missing QSU meetings all year, so you have yet to meet the angel Peter. Although I am sad to report that he just told me he has a boyfriend."

I hated to do this to Fred, except I didn't because he'd just been trying to get in my boyfriend's pants, so I put an arm around Peter's waist. "I know."

Peter said, "So you've already met my boyfriend, Logan."

Fred's mouth hung open comically for a moment, which felt like sweet justice. "What? How can you? How long?"

"We haven't been dating very long," I said, "but you could maybe stop macking on him."

Fred held his hands up. "If I had known." He squinted at us. "I don't know. I don't see it."

Peter put his arm around me. "Doesn't matter. Logan, will you dance with me?"

I figured I'd go back to pretending a life spent practicing music meant I understood rhythm and movement as it related to pop music, and I'd continue to swing my arms around awkwardly while Peter proved to the world he was the most beautiful man alive, but instead the opening bars of a slow ballad poured out of the DJ's speakers.

Oh boy.

Peter took me into his arms, so I put my hands on his shoulders. He swayed me back and forth until the song hit its chorus; then he pulled me close.

"Sorry about Fred," he said near my ear.

"You mean my former friend Fred?"

Peter laughed and it rumbled through his chest. "He didn't mean anything by it."

"I know," I said.

"I'm with you now."

"I know."

"Good."

I didn't know the song—my knowledge of pop music was severely limited—but the female singer had a nice voice, and the lyrics were romantic. Peter held me close and moved with me, and I held on as if he might slip away at any moment.

I realized something I'd thought was only lust had become so much more. I genuinely cared for him. I liked having him as my boyfriend.

I rested my head on his shoulder, and he held me tighter. If anyone here thought they could have him, they were learning now that he was mine.

As the song ended, he put a hand on my chin and pushed it up. Then he kissed me softly. The tempo changed back to a fast song, and some of the couples around us broke up as more single people moved onto the dance floor and groups formed. Peter didn't let go of me and kept swaying as if the slow song were still playing. Then he kissed me again. I felt like I was falling. Probably I was. I didn't even care that probably a bunch of people were watching us, because kissing him felt so good, and in his arms I felt safe and cared for and understood.

No one had ever really understood me. Not my friends, not my parents, not even Ellie. But Peter did. He got my anxiety about my career, he knew how fraught dealing with my parents could be, and he could see right through all my bullshit. I understood him now too, valued the things we had in common. I liked to think I got him as well as he got me. This dance was intended to be a safe space for us queer kids, but truthfully, I felt the most safe when I was with Peter.

He gently steered me off the dance floor but didn't let go of me. "It's hot out there," he said.

"I left my jacket over there at Noel and Dave's table."

He pulled away and took off his jacket. We walked together over to the table, and he slung the jacket over the chair next to mine. Then he leaned over and kissed my forehead. "Thanks."

"For what?"

"I know this whole dance thing is not your scene. But I'm having fun. Thank you for coming with me."

"I'm glad you're having fun. This is not terrible."

He laughed. "I'm going to get a drink. You want something?"

"A Coke or something would be good."

I watched Peter walk toward the bar, admiring the view. He looked so handsome in nice clothes, and on a more shallow level, his pants nicely highlighted his ass and thighs. He was a good-looking man, my Peter.

"You're really dating him?" said a voice off to the side. I turned to see Fred.

"Yeah. Only for a couple of weeks, but I like him."

"Of course. What's not to like? Sorry if I was an ass before. I honestly didn't know he was seeing anyone. How did you meet?"

"Funny story. Remember my homophobic roommate?" I explained about my misinterpreting things Peter said, and how my finally getting over myself and being straight with him led us to where we currently were.

"He's your roommate?" Fred asked, his eyes wide. "How do you ever get any homework done? Or, like, breathe regularly."

"I won't lie. It's been a struggle."

"What has been?" Peter asked as he walked back over. He handed me a plastic cup of soda.

"Fred asked how we met, so I was just explaining. It's a struggle to get anything done when you're around because you're distracting." I used my free hand to gesture at his chest.

Peter shot me a charming half smile. "A good distraction, I hope."

"Yeah. It is."

Fred rolled his eyes. "Oh God. I see it now. You're about to make out with each other. I'll leave you to it. And look, Jason just walked in. I heard he's still single, at least. When did everyone couple up?"

Peter and I laughed together as Fred left us. I really was having fun. I sipped my soda and looked up at my gorgeous boyfriend, who looked back at me, grinning.

CHAPTER 17

THE DINING hall in North Quad, where Peter and I lived, left something to be desired. It was a marvel of midcentury architecture, a squat two-story building made of beige bricks and wood. It was utilitarian inside: white walls, long folding tables and plastic chairs, a little salad bar that was always stocked with browning iceberg lettuce and shredded carrots. The other food wasn't much better; I don't think the menu had been updated since 1972.

When Peter and I went to eat there one evening about a week after the dance, they were serving this chicken and vegetable dish that had a few different names, as if the dining hall servers were trying to put one over on us. No, that's not sweet and sour chicken, it's mandarin chicken with vegetables. Either way, it was dry chicken, mushy vegetables, and some kind of vaguely sweet sauce that could very well have been squeezed out of duck sauce packets from the local Chinese restaurant.

I poked forlornly at it as Peter and I sat with a few of the Theater Club kids we'd run into. "I can't," I said.

Peter nodded. "This does seem especially sad late in the semester."

"They served chicken kiev yesterday," said Maggie with a shudder. "Do you know what that is? A chicken breast full of butter. It's like they want us to die of a heart attack. Or worse. When my boyfriend cut into it, butter spurted out and hit him in the eye."

This late in the semester, I felt obligated to use up some of my meal-plan card swipes, so I'd been encouraging Peter to come with me to the dining hall, but tonight's meal was truly gross. Since I didn't work—it might interfere with the study of violin, as my father often put it—my parents had me on a fairly generous allowance, but I doubted they'd be pleased to know I spent most of it on meals out instead of using the meal plan they purchased for me every semester.

I pushed some soggy red peppers around with my fork.

Peter jolted next to me and pulled his phone from his pocket. I contemplated the overcooked white rice ball on my plate. It had, of course, been placed there via ice cream scoop, so it was perfectly round, and was so sticky it hadn't lost its shape despite having chicken and vegetables and sauce poured on top of it.

Peter leaned over and whispered in my ear, "Dave, Noel, and Lily are at the Mac if you want to eat a real meal."

I wasn't sure that hamburgers and sandwiches prepared at WMU's main eatery/hangout spot constituted a "real meal," but it would surely be better than this. "Okay."

He turned to Maggie and her boyfriend. "Hey, we gotta go." I appreciated that he didn't even bother to explain. He stood, pulled on his coat, and waited for me to do the same. We said good-bye to our dinner companions, dumped our trays on the way out of the building, and then he took my hand and led me toward the center of campus.

It was cold. Well, it was December in Massachusetts. The air had a bite to it, and gusts of wind went right through my wool peacoat. Peter wore a navy blue ski parka that looked pretty toasty. He held my gloved hand as we walked the familiar paths past the FAC and Dickinson Hall and the library. I tried not to let the cold get to me.

Dave, Noel, and Lily were seated at a table in the middle of the Mac's dining area. We greeted them, and Peter installed me at the table.

"I'm really glad you texted. Thank you for rescuing us from the dining hall," Peter said. "It's orange chicken night."

Dave made gagging sounds. "Oh, I hate the magic chicken. I'm not sad to be off the meal plan. I'm happy we were able to help out."

"What do you want?" Peter asked me.

"Um. A turkey sandwich. With some chips?"

"Sure. Stay here. I'll get it."

"You want money?"

He waved his hand. "My treat."

My man was the best.

I'm sure I had a stupid smile on my face, but my friends were nice enough not to comment on it.

And they were my friends now. We chatted and they asked about classes, I asked them about the things they'd been up to, and we had an easy rapport. It was nice to be able to talk so freely about things that were not related to string instruments.

When Peter returned a few minutes later, Noel said, "Did you hear? The Theater Club settled on a show for next semester."

"Yeah?" Peter seemed excited.

"The year of Rodgers and Hammerstein continues. We're doing *The Sound of Music*." Noel glanced at Dave. "I'm going to audition for Captain von Trapp."

Noel's voice was too high of a tenor to pull off the role, but I decided to keep that to myself.

Peter had hearts in his eyes. "I always loved that show." He turned to me. "Can I tell you my favorite part?"

"When the nuns steal the car parts from the Nazis at the end so the von Trapps can get away?" I guessed.

Peter chuckled. "No. I always liked the romance in it. Maria is great because she stands up to the captain and she teaches his kids how to be children instead of soldiers. She's not fawning and simpering like the baroness. Von Trapp could fall in love with the beautiful, rich woman throwing herself at him, but instead he falls for Maria because she challenges him, you know? And then they sing to each other like they've found the key to the universe. I mean, that's love. In the movie when they sing 'Something Good,' that's my favorite."

I loved that he was this big, burly guy, but he was undone by a sweet romance in a movie musical. I leaned over and kissed his shoulder. "It was a different song in the original stage production, right?"

"I think so, yeah. Maybe I'll lobby for them to sing 'Something Good.'"

Lily sang the first few Maria lines from that song. She had a decent voice. Peter laughed with delight. "You should totally audition."

Lily shook her head. "Oh, no. Singing onstage? No. No. Please God, no."

"It's not like you're afraid of public speaking," Peter pointed out. "You talk in front of groups for the QSU all the time."

"Talk, yes. And I like bossing people around. I don't want to sing on a stage."

"Mark wanted to do *South Pacific*, but some of the club members were worried the show could be seen as racist." Noel sipped from a big paper cup.

"I think the opposite is true," Dave said. "The show confronts the racism of its day head-on, doesn't it? 'You've Got to Be Carefully Taught' is basically about how people are taught racism but aren't born with it. The racism of most of the characters gets challenged throughout the show."

"Yeah, but a couple of the Theater Club officers are really risk averse."

"Which is why you haven't gotten to do anything that might be 'controversial.'" Lily made finger quotes.

"Exactly," said Noel. "A bunch of us wanted to do *Hair* this semester, and even after the nude scene was ruled out, Jane and Maria thought the references to sex and drugs in the lyrics would make it look like we were endorsing those things."

"Didn't the theater department just do a production of a play that included characters casually snorting cocaine?" I asked. "I doubt anyone viewed it as an endorsement of cocaine use."

"When the theater department does it, it's art." Noel rolled his eyes.

"*The Sound of Music* is not a terrible choice," said Peter.

"There was some talk of doing a fundraiser early next semester in which we put on a bunch of scenes from various Rodgers and

Hammerstein shows." Noel picked up his cup and tilted it toward Peter. "I thought we could update them for the twenty-first century. Switch up gender and race in some cases. Like *Hamilton*, you know? Take these old songs from the forties and fifties and put modern spins on them."

"That's a cool idea." Peter sat up a little straighter. "I'd love to help out with something like that."

"We'd probably not do costumes, or we'd do simple costumes," said Noel. "Mark and Jane are worried about the lederhosen budget."

We all laughed.

"I'd love to help out too," I said. "If I can make it work with my schedule. If you need accompaniment, I mean. I play piano okay. Well enough to accompany singers, anyway, since the piano isn't really the star."

"You play piano too?" Peter asked with awe.

"Not as well as violin. One of my instructors in high school thought it would be useful to learn it, so I did. When I led rehearsals as concertmaster of my high school orchestra, I found it helpful sometimes to play a melody on the piano for the violins to hear. Sometimes it helps to hear the notes like that before playing it yourself."

"Is there anything you can't do?" Peter asked.

"There are a lot of things I can't do."

Peter's cell phone rang just then. The display said *Dad*. "I'd better get this." He grabbed his phone and walked out of the restaurant to a quieter spot. I watched him go, somewhat concerned. Probably a call from his father wasn't good news.

"So that's going well," Lily said when he was out of earshot.

"What?"

"You and Peter. Things seem to be going well between you. I saw you dancing together at the semiformal."

"Oh. Yeah." My face heated. "It's good. I think we've reached some kind of understanding."

"I like you guys as a couple."

I really appreciated that. "Thanks." I didn't know how sustainable our relationship was, but I was determined to enjoy it while it lasted. Often I was happy to bask in it, but sometimes doubts crept in. We were roommates, after all, and if anything went wrong, it could blow up in our faces. Changing dorm rooms was an incredibly difficult process, I'd heard, and I suspected "we dated and broke up" was not something the housing office would think was the sort of emergency they'd quickly accommodate.

I really tried not to assume the worst-case scenario would come true. I glanced back toward where my boyfriend spoke with his father on the phone. My heart reached out to him because I knew speaking to his father stressed him out. And I thought to myself that, as long as we continued to care for each other, we'd be all right.

THE NEXT day Noel came by my dorm while Peter was at the library. He wanted to get notes I had for a class I'd taken the semester before.

"It feels like such a cheat, this class," he said as I handed him my notes. He was taking a science class called The Physics of Music. "Normally it's not hard, but all the math in this last unit is making me dizzy. Thank you so much for the notes."

"Professor Clarkson puts all the formulas on the first page of the exam. If you can remember what the letters in the formulas represent, all you have to do is plug in the numbers."

"That's good to know. I'd prefer *not* to flunk the fake science class I'm taking to fill the gen ed requirement." Noel looked at my notes dubiously. He slid them into a folder in his bag, then looked up at me. "How are things going? You ready for the December concert?"

"Sure. As I'll ever be."

Noel regarded me carefully. "You don't sound so enthusiastic."

"No, I am. But, like, how do you feel before you go onstage for a Theater Club production?"

"Nervous. Worried I'll trip and fall on my face."

"Yeah. I feel that. Except I'm worried my finger will slip and I'll play a note flat. I'm worried I'll stumble over a note and everyone in the audience will know it. I'm worried that if I make one tiny mistake, I'll blow the whole concert. And I realize how crazy and irrational that is."

"But you can't help it." Noel sat in my desk chair. "I know. Last year, when we did *Guys and Dolls*? That was the first time I'd had a real part in a show instead of just being part of the ensemble. I was nervous as hell. It didn't help that I spotted Dave in the audience during the second show. We weren't dating yet, but I had a terrible crush on him. I spent half my time offstage, worried I would throw up."

There was something sweet about that, but it felt intrusive to comment on it, so I just said, "I'm a little nervous about the concert, and about the fact that scouts for orchestras are going to be there, and that my parents are going to be there, and that they have this whole plan for me that involves playing in a big orchestra after graduation. And I just... I don't know. I'll be fine once the concert starts." I sat at the foot of my bed. It seemed we were chatting. I was happy to have a friend, so I didn't mind Noel making himself at home.

He nodded slowly. "I don't want to tell you what to do, but I think there comes a time when you have to decide what you want and not what your parents want. Hell, if I did what my parents wanted, I'd still be in the closet, and I'd be studying something practical like business or a hard science." He sighed. "They couldn't stand having a gay son, so here I am, paying for my own psych degree."

I rubbed his shoulder. I heard what he was saying. I understood how lucky I was.

He sniffed. "It's better this way. I have the freedom to do what I want."

"I'm glad for that, at least. I just wish I knew what I wanted. A lot of times, I don't know."

Noel nodded. "Things with Peter are going well, though. At least I infer. He talks about you all the time."

I groaned aloud to hide the smile I felt stretching my lips. "Does he?"

"I don't think he realizes he's doing it. It'd be annoying if it weren't so cute."

"Well, gee."

Noel grinned.

"Things are going well. Really well. I'm worried it's clouding my judgment. Like, if I got an offer from an orchestra in LA or Chicago or, hell, even New York, I'd have a hard time taking it because it would move me away from Peter."

"Maybe that's your answer."

"But that's crazy, isn't it? We haven't been dating very long. I like him a lot, but I don't know yet if it's love or lust or what. Could be in two weeks we'll remember why we don't like each other and it will all blow up in our faces."

"Could be you'll live happily ever after." Noel giggled, probably recognizing how cheesy the line was. "Hey, you have at least another year of school, right? No rush to decide."

"That's true." I still felt uneasy.

"Look, I'll tell you something I've learned recently. Life is uncertain. You never know what's about to happen. Sometimes what feels like the worst turns out to be the best."

Noel looked away, toward some spot on Peter's side of the room, and although I didn't want to upset him, I wondered if something was bothering him. He seemed out of sorts. "Is everything okay?" I asked.

"Yeah." He nodded and rubbed his eyes. "Dave and I had this dumb fight last week. Total miscommunication."

Since mine and Peter's whole relationship had started with a miscommunication, I completely understood that. I nodded. "Been there."

Noel nodded. "We resolved it, but it just reminded me that I love him, and I know he loves me but I still doubt him sometimes."

This was about to get personal, and I hesitated to make him talk about it, but it also seemed like he'd opened a door. So I said, "Why do you doubt him?"

Noel glanced away again. "I don't know what Peter has told you about us."

"Hardly anything."

He nodded. "Dave and I met last semester. He was in the closet at the time. Well, 'in the closet' implies he even knew he was bi, which he didn't until after we met."

"Really?" I said.

"Really. We dated all summer, but he was terrified to come out to anyone. Do you have any idea how frustrating it is to date a guy in the closet?"

"I never have, but I can imagine."

Noel shifted his weight on the chair a little and played with the strap of his bag. "I didn't like that he could be so dishonest. He pulled me into the closet with him. So I broke up with him. I just couldn't stand it. After everything I went through with my family, I never wanted to hide who I was from anyone ever again." He dropped the strap of his bag and took a deep breath. "He came out to everyone after we broke up. We ran into each other at the beginning of this semester and he persuaded me to take him back. Don't get me wrong, I'm really glad I did. Best decision I made all semester. I love him and we have a great relationship."

"But you have doubts sometimes."

"Yeah. He was capable of that kind of dishonesty once, so maybe he could do something like that again. I don't really believe he would ever lie to me. But he might shade the truth, or keep something from me. In this case, he didn't, thankfully. I just misinterpreted something he said."

"You guys seem like such a solid couple." I liked watching them together when we hung out because they always seemed like they had the best time in each other's company.

"We are. Like I said, I don't regret taking him back. Most of the time I'm really happy. I'm just saying, not everything is perfect or predictable. And not just with relationships." He took a deep breath and looked at me. "I think we always have these expectations, you know? Each semester, we look at our course load, and we imagine what each class will be like. We take a new job with expectations. I work at a clothes store, and when customers come in, I try to guess what clothes they'll buy. I'm usually right, but sometimes I'm wrong. That's what I mean."

I wasn't completely sure I understood the larger point he was trying to make, but I nodded.

"I could have toed the line with my parents. I could have let them pay for my school while I stayed in the closet. But you know what? I would have been miserable."

I touched his hand, trying to be friendly.

He squeezed my fingers and let go. "We always have to make these decisions. Do what's expected of us or do what feels right. My parents disowned me, and that was the worst thing I've ever had to deal with. I'm stressed sometimes because I don't have that safety net. If my hours get docked at work or if some big expense comes up, I'm screwed. But at the same time? My life is so much better. I control my own life. I have my own apartment. And I'm in love with a great guy. I could have gone along with what my parents had expected and been unhappy, but instead I decided to take the riskier path. It's a lot more rewarding. Do you get what I'm saying?"

"Yeah, I think so." And I did. It spoke to what I'd been struggling with all semester. Following the path chosen for me versus forging my own path. "I'm really glad things are working out for you."

"Thank you. Things will work out for you too."

I wasn't completely convinced, but I could see how they might.

Noel's words stayed with me long after he left. Peter came home shortly afterward from a late-night study session at the library.

"I have so much knowledge in my brain right now," he said, seeming tired but happy. "I'm so going to ace this exam."

"Good. What's it in again?"

"My tax class."

We grimaced in mutual understanding of how Peter felt about taxes.

Peter was a risk. Things were good with us now, but we were young and a lot could happen in the next few months. There was no guarantee of a happily ever after here. We could break up, or have problems we couldn't solve, or betray each other in some way. But I was so happy when I was with him that maybe it was worth the risk.

Maybe what I really needed was to shake things up a bit. Not to be stuck in my routines. Not to do what people expected of me just because it was expected, but figure out what I really wanted and then pursue that.

"There you go with those gears behind your eyes again," Peter said. "What are you thinking?"

"Oh, nothing important. Noel was here earlier and we talked and I was just thinking about something he said."

"Is it between you, or are you willing to share?"

Peter had probably heard all about Noel and Dave, since they were both really Peter's friends more than mine, but I still didn't want to betray Noel's confidence. "I mentioned that I wasn't sure what I'd do if I got an offer to play in an orchestra that made me move across the country, and how, like, that could take me away from you. Which would completely suck, by the way."

Peter sat next to me on my bed. "That would suck, I agree. Is it a real concern?"

"Who the hell knows? And either way, it's still three semesters away, so I'm trying not to worry about it yet, but it's hard to overcome my essential nature, you know?"

He laughed, because of course he did know. He kissed the top of my head. "So that's something we'll worry about when it happens."

"You expect to still be with me in a year and a half?"

He put an arm around me. "Of course. Stop being so pessimistic."

"Again, essential nature."

"Like I said, we'll figure it out. Work hard to overcome your essential nature. You want some distraction?" He ran a hand over my back and raised an eyebrow.

"Anytime," I said. Then I kissed him.

CHAPTER 18

I SAT with Dave and a couple of his friends in the audience for *Oklahoma!* We were at the last performance, which was on a Saturday. I'd felt a little bad about not going to opening night—or every performance, for that matter—especially after Peter had scored a couple of free tickets for me, but after I'd missed rehearsal for the semiformal, I didn't think Costner would be pleased if I missed any more.

Even though I remembered that Noel had said his boyfriend was a theater queen, Dave looked like such a jock that I still felt some surprise when he launched into a lecture on Rodgers and Hammerstein while we waited for the curtain to rise. His friend Kareem made a quacking duck gesture with his hand a lot through this particular talk, like he'd heard it before. Most of Dave's talking points were things I already knew too, but I wanted his friendship, so I humored him.

"There's a filmed version of the show with Hugh Jackman," I said. "I think it's a West End cast from the '90s. They have it for rent at the library. If you want to see a production with maximum eye candy, I mean."

Dave found this hilarious.

I chuckled with him until the house lights dimmed.

The show was fun. I spent a good half of it trying to spot Peter in the wings. He popped out every time the black-clad tech crew came out to change a set. While that did distract me from some parts of the show, I also kept an eye on Ellie playing in the pit and everyone I knew onstage. Ellie looked great, and also like she was having a lot of fun. Noel was very good as Will Parker, although he sang better than he acted. He wasn't that believable as a straight man in love with a woman, and he and the other men really camped up "It's a Scandal! It's a Outrage!" The dream ballet at the end of Act I was pretty bonkers, but in a really wonderful way. The whole second act reminded me how crazy the plot of this show was, but the look on Dave's face indicated he was eating it up. I thought it was fun. Watching it made me miss playing with this group. I wanted to be in Ellie's seat in the pit. I wanted to be the one with a little solo during the dream ballet.

As significant others of the cast and crew, Dave and I had been invited to the cast party at the Pub after the show. We hung around in the lobby, chatting with Kareem and Dave's friends; then I led Dave out to my car. We beat most of the Theater Club members to the restaurant. Dave was twenty-one and got a coveted neon pink bracelet. I wasn't much of a drinker, so it didn't faze me much, and I was happy to drink iced tea while Dave sipped a beer. We chatted about the show while waiting for our boyfriends.

Dave was the sort of guy I never would have been friends with if fate hadn't kept throwing us together; besides musical theater, his obsessions included sports, particularly baseball, and movies, two things I knew almost nothing about. So we didn't have a lot in common to talk about beyond people we knew and the show we'd just seen, but Dave seemed like a genuinely good guy, so I didn't mind.

The pit orchestra arrived first. Ellie gave me a big hug, and I introduced her to Dave. "What'd you think?" she asked.

"It was a great show. Everyone was fantastic. Listening to the pit made my fingers a little itchy. I wished I could have played with you."

"Me too. It's not the same without you."

"Maybe next semester." I decided I'd figure out how to make it happen. Maybe it was time to stick up for myself more. No more sanity-challenging extra rehearsals. I'd spend Friday nights with Peter instead of at the FAC. "You all sounded great, though. Really."

She smiled. "Thanks."

Everyone else kind of trickled in after that. The actors with the least elaborate costumes and makeup showed up first. Noel arrived in the middle of the pack and beelined for us when he came in. He gave Dave a big kiss. Dave gushed about how great he was. They both had stars in their eyes. It was sweet to see two guys so into each other.

It surprised me that I didn't feel a pang of jealousy like I usually did when I saw happy couples. Perhaps because I had Peter now.

Peter was one of the last people to arrive at the party, probably because he was overseeing cleanup at the theater. He looked tired but happy when he found his way to me. He had to travel a gauntlet through the restaurant; everyone wanted to shake his hand or hug him. But he finally got to me and just beamed. So I hugged him and kissed his cheek and congratulated him on the show.

"Thanks," he said softly, hugging me back. "I'm glad you guys came tonight."

"Yeah, this was far and away our best performance," said Noel. He'd changed out of his costume into a simple—for Noel—gray sweater and dark pants, but he still had a fair amount of stage makeup on his face. Most prominent was the eyeliner and blush, which was not to mention the freckles someone had drawn on him. I wasn't sure of the reasoning there, beyond that someone maybe thought they added to his character's "aw, shucks" charm.

"I agree. Everyone was on their game tonight," said Peter.

"Have you heard yet what you're doing next semester?" Ellie snagged some kind of meat on a stick thing as a waiter went by with a tray.

"*Sound of Music*," said Noel.

"Oh, I love *Sound of Music*." Ellie held her hands over her heart.

"It's a popular choice. I'd still love to see you all do something edgy." Peter held his hands out as if he were trying to mime edginess.

"Half the Club wants to do something like *Hamilton*," Noel said, "but given how white we are, we'd never pull it off. Well, that, and we can't get performance rights yet."

"What about *Rent*?" Peter asked.

"Probably next it'll be *Carousel*." Ellie crossed her arms and raised her eyebrows.

I wouldn't have been mad if it was. After that party Peter had dragged me to, I'd listened to the cast recording a couple of times in my rare moments of spare time. I'd particularly liked a few lines from "What's the Use of Wond'rin." Because what was the use of wondering if things would work out, if he was the right guy for me, if we'd be happy? He was my feller, as the song went, and I cared for him. That was all there was to that. I sang softly, mostly to myself, but I projected those lines loud enough for Peter to hear.

Peter looked at me like I'd just put the sun in the sky. He put an arm round me and hugged me close. "Regardless, I think *The Sound of Music* will be fun."

I spent the rest of the party hanging on Peter, and not even in a territorial way, just because I liked being near him. He didn't seem bothered. He kept grabbing my hand or my shoulder and kissing the top of my head. He kept introducing me to people as "my boyfriend, Logan," which made my heart skip every time.

When we went up to the bar to get fresh drinks, he said, "You really liked the show?"

"I did. I enjoyed it."

Peter nodded. "I know I didn't have *that* much to do with it, since I'm not an actor or whatever." He looked down with a frown.

"The sets looked amazing. Did you do a lot of the painting?"

That seemed to put some spark back into him. "Yeah, the background with the wheat stalks and the barn in the background? That's what I was painting when I fell and sprained my ankle. And the barn interior, I painted that too."

"You're really talented." It wasn't a lie. The sets had looked professional. And for a production put on by a club that had almost no money, that was saying something. "Everything moved like clockwork too. You had a lot to do with that."

He smiled. "Thank you. I really tried. I love this stuff."

"I know." I took his hand. "I could see you being a set designer for Broadway or something like that."

His smile widened. "Oh my God. I would die. That would be amazing." Then his face fell a little.

"I know all about your parents," I said, "but we're young. I think we still have to dream. The arts are hard to fund, so maybe you do follow your plan, do the green visor thing for a while, then pursue set design, or make movies, or design magazines, or anything you want."

"The green visor thing?"

"Number crunching. Taxes. The accountant thing."

He hugged me. "Do you know why accountants wore visors?"

"They're a hot fashion trend?"

"Everyone who had to stare at text a lot under the harsh lights in the early part of the twentieth century—not just accountants, but copy editors, telegraph operators, that kind of thing—they wore those visors to help curb eyestrain. Then someone invented a better light bulb and accountants stopped wearing the green shades, except on TV. And in your imagination apparently." He softly tapped my forehead.

"I'm just saying. There are worse plans. I'd like to see you doing something that made you as happy as building those sets clearly did." I put my arms around him.

He rubbed my back. "You're sweet. I never would have guessed that when we first met."

"I mean, it's hopeless and everything is terrible."

He laughed. "Too late. I know the truth now, Logan."

THAT NIGHT, when we arrived back at our room, we took off our clothes and settled into my bed as if by some unspoken agreement. I rolled into him and said, "I'm ready."

He stroked my weird hair. "For what?"

I'd been postponing penetrative sex. It wasn't that I held the act sacred, and I'd bottomed for guys before, but I'd wanted it to have meaning with Peter. He was the first guy I'd ever felt this strongly about, and he was my boyfriend, so I didn't want it to be cheap or routine. But after the night we'd had, how close to him I felt after being paraded around the party as his boyfriend, I wanted to give him something important. "I want you inside me," I whispered.

He kissed me fiercely. "Are you sure?"

"Yeah. You're... I want to be close to you."

He stroked my hair and met my gaze. He understood why this moment was important. "Yes. I want that too."

"There are condoms in the top drawer of my nightstand."

I couldn't reach it, but Peter could. I'd bought them the week before, thinking we might arrive at this moment soon. He rolled away from me, dug through the drawer, and returned holding a condom. He showed it to me and kissed me again. "I know how much this means," he said.

I ran a hand down his arm. I knew he'd understand me. I kissed him. "Thank you."

He hovered over me, smiling. "This will be good, I promise."

I had to smile back. "I believe you."

He was so beautiful. He stroked my hair, ran his hands down my chest, gazed at my body as if he were committing it to memory. His big, warm hands moved over me. I reached up to touch his hair, played with it a little. Our eyes met. I imagined I could see everything he felt for me in his eyes, and his gaze was intense, but most of what I saw was how blue his eyes were in the dim light of our dorm room. He bent his head to kiss me again, and I wrapped my hand around the base of his head to keep him there.

"Spread your legs," he whispered.

I did. I wanted to be with him this way. I loved just being naked with him in bed like this, but I was ready for something more. The simple idea of him being inside me was something that felt special to me. It wasn't the act itself, it was *this man.*

He took his time. He told me there was no rush. He took care of me, preparing me slowly, kissing my lips or my chest or my face as he did so.

"You are so fucking hot," he said. "I want you so bad."

"You can have me."

He slipped a finger inside me, and my heart sped up in anticipation. "You're amazing, Logan."

I liked listening to him sing my praises, but I thought that if he was still capable of speaking complete sentences, I had to do more. I wrapped my hand around his hard cock and stroked while he touched me, preparing my body. He groaned, lightly biting my shoulder. I writhed against his hands. He knew exactly where to touch me, how to make my body come alive. We kissed more and touched each other everywhere, and my heart raced. I kissed him and bucked against him and was rewarded when he started mumbling nonsense in my ear.

When he finally hovered over me, his hips cradled between my legs, I was crazy with lust, and I begged him to please push inside me. I felt the blunt head of his cock poking softly at my skin and I shifted my hips, trying to encourage him. He kissed my face.

"Calm," he said, panting a little. "I'm trying to savor this moment."

"God, Peter. I want… please…."

He kissed me hard. Then he finally pressed forward.

The feeling of him inside me, stretching me, was intense, and brought my focus to the place where our bodies joined. He felt huge, and it burned, but it was good too, and my own cock bobbed happily as he moved in me. Being this close to him felt heady and hot. We kissed as he slowly pumped in and out of my body, and as my blood rushed and I felt us crashing toward climax, I knew we'd taken a turn in our relationship, that something between us had grown and changed. He and his big body surrounded me, in the best way. I put my arms around him too, pulled him to me, pushed against him. I stroked his hair, his back, tried to touch every part of him, wanted to commit this moment to memory. My eyes stung a bit, as if I were crying, though I wasn't, more struck by an intense wave of emotion, of adoration, of glee that I was sharing this moment with Peter. And when I came, it was such a relief I nearly cried. He kissed my cheeks over and over, as if he were kissing away the unshed tears, and then he thrust into me one more time, wrapped his arms around me, and came on a long groan. He kept kissing me all over as we came down together. Neither of us seemed to want to move. Because we were together.

He took care of the condom and settled back into bed with me. He smoothed my hair out of my face and said, "You're perfect. You know that?"

I blurted out a surprised laugh. "Hardly."

He kissed my forehead. "Well, not *perfect*. But you've been much less uptight lately, and I really enjoy being with you. So let's settle for 'you're pretty awesome.'"

"Okay. You too." And maybe he was right; being with Peter, making new friends, all of that made me happier than I'd been in… well, since I could remember. Probably I was less tense, pending concert notwithstanding. Maybe it was time to make some changes.

He pulled me closer. "So I guess if you came to see *Oklahoma!* I should come see your concert next week."

I groaned. "Don't feel like you have to. Really."

"No, I want to. I'd like to hear you play. You told me when I moved in here that you practice in the room sometimes, but I've never heard you play solo."

"I don't like practicing in front of people."

"Do you not want me to come to the concert?"

"No, I do. Definitely. I'd love it if you were there. But I want you to go because you want to, not because you feel obligated."

He smiled. "I want to."

I smiled back.

I fell asleep that night thinking about how much things had changed in just the space of a couple of months. I liked the changes. I wanted things to change more.

CHAPTER 19

I HAD some concert-night jitters. This was pretty common; I often got nervous right before I performed, but usually once I was onstage and had played the first note, the nerves melted away. I tuned my violin at a piano backstage while I waited for Costner to give us the go-ahead to assemble onstage. He came over and patted me on the back.

"I've got friends in the audience," he said.

By which he meant there were orchestra scouts sitting out there. That compounded my nerves. Knowing my parents and Peter were in the audience too wasn't helping. I played middle A on the piano, tuned my A string, and then pressed a hand on top of the piano, suddenly dizzy.

"You all right?" Costner asked.

"A little nervous."

He handed me a digital tuner. "That piano's a little flat. Use this. And you'll be fine. You know this music well. This is your fifth concert with the WMU orchestra, so this is old hat now."

"Yeah. I know."

He nodded. I placed the tuner on the piano's music stand and used it to tune my violin, after which time Costner took it back and went to find someone else to pester.

We got the signal to go out onstage a minute later. WMU orchestra procedure was for everyone to walk onto the stage in random order and proceed to their seats. I waited in the wings while everyone walked out. Ellie patted my arm on her way past me, and we nodded at each other. Once every seat was occupied, I walked out. The audience applauded, but I barely heard it. I stood for a moment, waiting for the applause to die out; then I sat and played a middle A for the violins to tune with. When they finished,

I played again for the brass and woodwinds. When they finished and all was silent, Costner walked out onstage.

We played eight pieces in all, with the Bach concerto as our grand finale. As predicted, once the concert got started, I stopped feeling nervous and focused on the music. It was hard to tell what was really happening from inside the orchestra, but to my ear, we collectively sounded very good, and I didn't make any major mistakes. I could have picked the performance apart—the second violins played part of a Handel concerto a smidge flat, the clarinets came in half a beat too early in a different piece, and so on—but I forced myself to stop focusing on what had happened and instead concentrate on what I needed to do. A lot of muscle memory got involved; I'd played this music so many times that I could do it without thinking very hard. In fact, during the less complicated parts, my mind wandered. I thought about Peter, about my parents, about the scouts in the audience, about what I really hoped the outcome of this concert would be.

Peter in a house in the Berkshires. That's what I really wanted.

The concert wrapped up. Costner made me stand up first. I turned toward the audience and forced myself to soak up the applause, because I hated this part of it. I felt awkward and a little naked standing up there onstage with a thousand people looking at me. I was glad when Costner invited the rest of the orchestra to stand, diverting everyone's attention. Finally we filed offstage and I took a deep breath.

"Excellent," Costner said, walking up to me. He shook my hand. "Fantastic. Really wonderful, Logan."

"Thank you."

I walked over to where I'd stashed my violin case. Ellie followed me and gave me a hug once I put my instrument down. "That was brilliant," she said. "Best I've ever heard you play."

"Yeah?"

"Yeah. I think all those extra rehearsals paid off. I'm sure one of the scouts will invite you to play for them."

"I doubt it. I'm just a junior. I have three semesters of school to finish. No one's going to ask me." My heart still raced a bit from the thrill of performing, so I took a few calming breaths and said, "I thought the whole orchestra sounded good. How do you think the whole thing went?"

"Really well! I got that sixteenth-note pattern in the Bach that I've been struggling with all the semester. Finally nailed it, like, a week ago."

"It's a tough pattern."

"Like that Handel thing we did last year. Took me forever to master it, but I finally got it right before the concert. I was worried I'd mess it up tonight, but I got it. And the violins stayed in tune, at least from what I could hear."

"From where I sat too. We do always pull it together in the end, don't we?"

"I mean, it wasn't *perfect*. But it was pretty good."

We packed up side by side, Ellie chattering on about imperfections she'd noticed in the performance, because she was as sharp and obsessive as I was: the cellos came in a half beat late in one of the pieces but quickly corrected it; one of the oboes was a wee bit sharp, and so on. Normally I would have joined her and critiqued the orchestra. It was hard not to finish a concert without making at least a couple of small mistakes, the kinds of things 99 percent of the audience likely hadn't even picked up on but that we all knew hadn't been quite right. Now, however, I only half listened, anxious about my parents and Peter waiting for me in the lobby.

"Your family come?" I asked Ellie.

"Yeah, they drove out from Fall River. We're going to dinner after. You want to join us?"

"Thank you, but I already ate. Plus I have to worry about the fact that my parents and my boyfriend are both in the audience and about to meet for the first time."

Ellie raised an eyebrow. "Peter's your boyfriend now?"

"Yeah, we… yeah." I couldn't keep the smile off my face. "Whatever. Let's not make it a big thing. We only really started calling each other that a few weeks ago."

She punched my arm lightly. "And you didn't tell me?"

"I… I've been busy."

"Busy making out with Peter, from the sounds of it." She punched my arm again. "You guys are so cute."

I rolled my eyes.

Ellie and I walked through a side corridor to the lobby, where a lot of people were gathered. Ellie's parents, not new to this, were waiting for her right near the door we walked through. My parents weren't far behind them. I looked across the lobby and spotted Peter talking to Noel on the far side of the lobby.

Ellie's parents each hugged and congratulated me. I spoke with them for a minute so as not to be rude, but was pretty glad when my father walked over to rescue me.

My father was a barrel-chested man who resembled Pavarotti a little if I squinted, and my mother looked elegant next to him, wearing a simple black dress with gold accents, with her coat slung over her arm. "Hello, sweetheart," my mother said, kissing my cheek and ruffling my hair. I tried to finger-comb it back into place as my dad shook my hand.

I spent the next five minutes trying to make eye contact with Peter so he'd walk over to me while my parents, Costner, the other musicians, and random strangers all praised me. I awkwardly accepted their praise.

Finally Peter and Noel seemed to catch on that I wasn't capable of moving across the lobby with all these people talking to me, and they started walking forward. The butterflies that had flitted around my stomach before the concert were back with a vengeance.

"Um, Mom? Dad? I need you to meet someone."

My mother seemed to catch on quickly. My father was happily oblivious. He shook hands with Costner and praised his work. When Peter got close enough to me to hug, I held a hand up and gestured toward my parents with my eyes. No hugs with them so close. Peter nodded.

To my mother, and loud enough for my father to hear, I said, "This is my friend Noel. And this is my boyfriend. Peter. Peter, this is my mom. The guy with the beard is my dad."

Peter nodded and shook my mother's hand. "Nice to meet you, Mrs. Miller."

I hated this. My stomach churned. It wasn't even that I wanted my parents' approval, but I had this nagging fear that my mother would take one look at Peter and... I didn't know. Take him away from me. But I needed Peter. He made me happy in a way I rarely had been. And the irrational part of my brain cooked up a scenario in which my performance tonight was just flawed enough that my mother would declare my dating was too much of a distraction.

Peter must have sensed my distress, because he reached over and briefly touched my hand.

My mother gave Peter a long look. "Of course. Peter. Logan mentioned you at Thanksgiving. Did you enjoy the concert?"

"I did." Peter sounded hesitant, like he was afraid to answer lest he say the wrong thing. I couldn't blame him. My mother was intimidating as hell.

My father came over and shook Peter's hand. "Logan's boyfriend, huh?" He sounded deeply skeptical.

"Yeah, Dad. We've been dating about a month. I would have waited to introduce you, but since you're all here." I gestured at the group.

"Are you a musician?" Dad asked.

"Accounting major," said Peter, glancing at me.

"Ah, that's a solid career path. Logan is going to make music for the world, but we need accountants too. I work at the Bank of Western Mass in Springfield, so I know all about that."

"I'm sorry," I mouthed to Peter. He nodded faintly.

I wanted my parents to leave. We'd had dinner before the concert because my father had a thing about eating dinner early, as if he were seventy instead of forty-nine. I wanted to go back to my room with Peter and hide there until everyone in the universe forgot about this concert and stopped wanting to talk to me about it.

"I am really proud of you, Logan," my mother said. "You looked great up there tonight. Sounded beautiful."

"Professor Costner picked a great program," said Dad. Then he lowered his voice. "He said there were a lot of scouts in the audience."

"He told me the same," I said.

"This could mean big things for you, son."

I nodded. I didn't want to discuss it further.

"Maybe before the end of the semester, we can take Peter to dinner," Mom said. "Get to know him better. If you're serious about this boy, of course."

"He's standing right here, Mom. And yes, I'm serious."

I might as well have told her I'd started snorting cocaine. Her expression went sour, but she nodded. "We'll call you, okay? Set up a time. But don't let it take away from your music or your studies."

"I won't."

"I'm your mother. I worry about you."

She worried I wouldn't fulfill her dreams, more like. If she was legitimately worried about my welfare, her presence here probably wouldn't be causing me this much anxiety. But I said, "I know."

My parents hugged me, reminded me to call them, and took their leave around the same time Ellie exited with her parents for a late dinner. That left me with Peter, Noel, and the remaining stragglers in the lobby.

"Your parents are intense," said Noel.

"I know. I'm sorry."

"Not your fault." Peter looked shell-shocked, but he squeezed my hand. "Did you drive?"

"No. Mom and Dad picked me up while you were at the gym. Then they just abandoned me here." I sighed. "We can walk. It's fine."

"I can see if Dave's around." Noel pulled his phone out of his pocket and fiddled with it as he spoke. "I was going to take the bus home, but if he's around, maybe he can drive you up the hill before he drives me home."

"Don't make him go out of his way."

"He has a test tomorrow. He might be at the library."

As Noel texted Dave, I hugged Peter. I rested my head on his shoulder and inhaled his scent. He always smelled a little minty—he used some kind of fancy soap—but tonight he smelled like something more. Maybe cologne. He was dressed nicely too, in a crisp blue dress shirt and gray trousers. Like he'd wanted to impress someone. Maybe my parents.

"Dave's at his place in North Amherst," Noel said.

"We can walk up the hill in less time than it will take him to get here. It's fine, Noel."

"Are you sure? It sucks that your parents abandoned you."

I suspected that Noel related to that better than anyone, but I shrugged. His parents had actually disowned him. Mine had just driven back to Springfield. They only objected to my being gay insofar as it might interfere with my study of music. "It's okay. I want to walk. And I've got my big strong man to keep me safe." I nudged Peter with my elbow.

Noel smiled. "All right."

We walked Noel to the bus stop; then Peter and I started up the hill, hand in hand. The walk from the FAC to our dorm was short but all uphill, over a paved path lined with trees. I did this trip many times a week and had for the two and a half years I'd been at WMU, but I saw it in a new way as I walked slowly, holding my boyfriend's hand. The moon and an occasional streetlight illuminated our way, and the night was quiet. Romantic.

"I never knew you were so talented," Peter said. "I mean, I knew you must have been to be concertmaster. You practice so much that all those hours have to add up to something. I knew intellectually you must be gifted, but to see you play was something else."

"Oh," I said.

"I mean, it was really amazing." He paused and dipped his head. "Sexy, even."

"Yeah?"

"Yeah. You kind of sway and shimmy when you play. Like a dancer. Did you know that?"

"Yes, although no one's ever put it that way."

"Seriously, though. I'm a little intimidated."

"I'm still the same guy I was yesterday. And I wasn't good enough to get into Juilliard. There are hundreds of kids right now who are even better than me who I'll be competing for orchestra spots with when I graduate."

"Really? I can't believe that."

"It's true. And I... I don't love competition. I just want to play. I love playing. But the rest of it?"

"I get that. If I could sing or play an instrument, I'd do it in a heartbeat. One of the things I love about the Theater Club is that there's no pressure, you know? It's not like the drama students who are trying to get acting jobs after college. Everyone is just there to have fun."

"That's what I always liked about playing in the pit orchestra. But, you know, nothing can detract from the music." I imbued a fair amount of sarcasm but added, "I rolled my eyes just then, in case it's too dark to see me."

Peter chuckled. "I don't really know much about classical music. But you definitely don't suck."

"That's a hell of an endorsement."

"You're sure you don't want to be in an orchestra?"

I groaned. "I don't know anything anymore. I mean, sure, I've fantasized about playing on a big stage with a famous orchestra. If the New York Philharmonic asked me to play with them tomorrow, I'd have a hard time turning them down. But it's such a long shot, and I don't think it's really sustainable as a career. I mean, you saw my mom tonight. Me succeeding in music is all she can think about. She doesn't care what I want."

"What do you want?"

"I want my little house in the Berkshires, and the husband, and the dog, and hell, maybe a couple of kids. I want… quiet. I want stability. I want to play for fun, not because I'm pressured into it."

"It's so funny. I always wanted instability. I want the risk and reward of being an artist, but instead I'm studying for a really mundane career. You want the opposite. Maybe the best spot is in the middle."

"It's why I haven't quit yet."

Peter squeezed my hand. "You've still got a little time to figure it out, right? It's not like you have to figure it out tomorrow."

"True," I said.

CHAPTER 20

WHEN I arrived at my one-on-one workshop with Costner the following week, there was a dark-haired man sitting in the room. He had a wealthy vibe to him; his suit looked expensive, his hair was combed just so, and his beard had been so neatly trimmed I thought it might have been drawn on.

Costner said, "Hi, Logan. I want to introduce you to Klaus Lundberg. We played in the Boston Pops together, what, ten years ago? Fifteen?" He looked at Mr. Lundberg for confirmation.

"Yes. I now work for a production company in Berlin." Lundberg had a soft accent like he'd been born in Europe—Germany, probably—but had spent enough time either traveling or living in the States that most of his speech had assimilated.

"Okay." I set my case on a chair. "Nice to meet you."

"Klaus is organizing an orchestral tour of Europe." Costner walked toward me and dropped a sheaf of sheet music on a music stand.

I started to cotton on to why Klaus was here, but decided to play dumb, because this was not what I wanted. Maybe I was wrong, but I feared I was right and I was about to get the offer that would thrill my parents.

"I am assembling an orchestra of talented musicians from North America to tour Europe next year, starting in February. You, Mr. Mitchell, are an amazing musician, and I believe you'd fit right into the orchestra I've assembled so far. Our concertmaster is Anthony Burke. Do you know him?"

I knew Tony, all right. He was a violin prodigy from Boston; we'd played in regional youth orchestras all through high school, and he'd somehow managed to show up at every one of my college admissions auditions. He had, of course, gone to Juilliard, just as my parents wanted for me. Tony was better than I was, though. I didn't feel much animosity toward him, beyond that his constant presence as the guy who was just a little better than I was got grating after a while. I hadn't actually thought of him in a year or two. Strange that he'd walk back into my life now.

"I know Tony Burke, yeah."

"I thought you might since you're both gifted musicians about the same age. I've signed on a number of other string players as well, from all over the US and Canada, plus a horn player from Mexico."

"Sounds nice." I had no idea what to say. My head was spinning. I knew he wanted me to join this orchestra, and the very thought of it made me nauseous.

Lundberg continued, "This orchestra will tour Europe for eight months, and in that time, you'd have the opportunity to meet with directors from other European orchestras. I happen to know there are orchestras in Vienna, Milan, and Barcelona that are currently recruiting, so this is a good way to get in front of their directors."

Wait, Vienna? Barcelona? I'd often imagined I'd move to New York or Boston after college; it was expected, though it didn't thrill me. But moving to Europe, possibly indefinitely if I got a spot at a European orchestra? And doing it starting in February? "What about the rest of school?"

"Talent matters more than the degree," Costner said. "This is an amazing opportunity. I think you'd fit in well with this orchestra, and Klaus knows a lot about putting on a show."

"I used to work on Vanessa-Mae's concerts," said Klaus. "Those were an incredible amount of fun."

I just stood there and stared, feeling flabbergasted.

"I know you were hoping for an orchestra in Boston," said Costner. "But you're young. This is an opportunity to travel. See the world. It'll be incredible."

I slid my violin case off my shoulder and placed it carefully on one of the chairs scattered throughout the room. "So you think I should drop out of college to tour with this orchestra?"

Costner shook his head. "I'm sure WMU would defer your last three semesters, if that's what you're worried about. The university would appreciate the prestige of having a student who was a world-renowned musician. You can tour with Klaus's orchestra and then finish your degree."

I doubted WMU would be that excited to have me back if I dropped out. It wasn't like I would be leaving to go star in a movie. Outside of a small circle of devotees, few cared about classical music. Most people couldn't name a single violinist, and if they did, it was a soloist. They remembered Joshua Bell. They remembered David Garrett. They would remember Tony Burke. They did not remember the kid who sat in the fourth row of violins. So I could run off to Europe, and then what? Move to Milan? Come back to the States, to nothing? Eight months on a tour of Europe sounded nice, but would it really mean anything for my career? To WMU? To future orchestras?

Not that I wanted fame. I just wanted to play. But suddenly I could see this tour ending and my being stranded in Europe and the vision of my little house in Massachusetts fading in the background as I spent the rest of my life fighting with talented musicians to sit in the back row of some orchestra in, like, Dresden or Helsinki or wherever.

I didn't want it. "I'm really honored by the offer. It sounds like an amazing program."

"Great!" Klaus clapped his hands once, as if the decision were made. "There's some paperwork to fill out and—"

I held up my hand. "Can I think about it? I hear what you're saying, but I really think I should talk to my parents before I give up school." This was, of course, a lie. My parents would have told me to take the orchestra gig. But I wanted some time to make sure it was something I wanted, or that wouldn't make me miserable, before I said yes.

"Of course." Costner fiddled with the music stand. "I know we sprung this on you. It must be a surprise. Take some time, talk it over with your parents, then let me know and I'll put you in touch with Klaus."

"Not too much time," said Klaus. "I need to have the lineup finalized by the end of the year."

"Which won't be a problem if Logan decides by the end of the semester."

They nodded at each other. My stomach churned. I didn't know how I'd get through a rehearsal with Costner now that I knew this.

Costner shuffled the music on the stand and then seemed to find what he was looking for. "This really is an amazing opportunity. I encourage you to take advantage of it." He slapped me on the back. "Let's show Klaus some of what you can do. That Mendelssohn piece you've been working on, let's start there."

I WALKED back to my dorm room after practice, feeling a great weight on my shoulders.

What I wanted was to spend time with Peter, to play in the pit of the next Theater Club musical, to enjoy my senior year of college. I knew there were hundreds of kids who would have killed to get an opportunity like the one I'd just been offered. Touring Europe had some appeal, and a lot of the cities Klaus had named were places I wanted to visit. Someday. The idea of going to Europe *now* overwhelmed me. But I could do it. I could also postpone leaving school, pass up this opportunity, and hope that somewhere less far from home had a spot for me a year from now. I could also say *fuck expectations* and start applying to education master's programs.

I had no idea what to do, and the decision was eating away at my insides. My parents really had put a lot of time and money into me and my violin. Well, violins. I owned three. I had my everyday practice violin, which was the one I hauled around with me most of the time. My concert piece was an antique—not a Stradivarius or anything like that, but a gorgeous violin made in Germany in the nineteenth century that made amazing sound. It hadn't been cheap; we'd paid for it in installments. And I had the cheap student violin I'd played once I'd graduated from the half-size one loaned to me when I'd first started to play, though it mostly stayed at my parents' house.

And it was because I loved all of my violins still that balking at Klaus Lundberg's offer didn't seem like an option. Because I did love to play, and there was still something appealing about playing in Europe. I probably would never get another opportunity like this. Costner was right, now was the time to do it, before I got older and had other obligations.

It was getting cold out. My breath puffed out in clouds as I walked up the hill. My knit gloves weren't quite getting the job done, and I clapped my hands a few times to get circulation going enough to warm up the tips of my fingers. I worried about the violin strapped to my back, how much the extreme cold would warp the wood, would knock it out of tune.

I'd been playing for as long as I could remember. The last fifteen years of my life—three-quarters of my time on earth—had been devoted to this instrument. I had dreams about sixteenth-note patterns. I had calluses on my fingers. I probably smelled like rosin most of the time. I could change a string on my violin in less time than it took some people to tie their shoes. I was constantly finding bow hairs stuck to my clothing. Next to the condoms in my bedside drawer were extra strings and bridges and my spare shoulder rest.

I lived and breathed violin. I would never give it up.

The real question was whether I wanted to play across Europe.

Peter was out when I got back to the room. I wanted to talk to him about all this, but instead I put my violin away and called my parents.

I explained the offer, the time frame, the trek across Europe. I explained how unlikely I thought it was that WMU would let me go and come back. Well, maybe they would; I couldn't know without asking. Either way, leaving school would draw out how long it took me to finish my BFA. Still, surprising no one, my mother said, "You're taking the spot, aren't you?"

"You don't think I should finish school before I run off to Europe? Normal parents would want me to finish school."

"I'm not a normal parent," Mom replied. "This is what you've wanted for so long. I'm supporting your dreams."

Uh-huh. "I just don't know, Mom. Something about this doesn't feel right."

"Don't tell me it's because you want to stay with your boyfriend. We discussed this. You can't let a boy get in the way of your career."

"That's not what's happening here." Peter was certainly a factor, but he wasn't the *only* factor. "I just don't feel ready to leave school yet. I want to finish my degree before I go play for an orchestra."

"You don't need a degree to play violin."

What my mother was saying was essentially *Fuck normal*, but I wanted some kind of normality after all. Thinking about Europe made my stomach twist. But would passing it up be a huge mistake?

"I'm just telling you what happened," I said. "Professor Costner said I have until the end of the semester to decide. That's still a couple of weeks away. So let me think about it, okay?"

"Okay, but you should really consider this offer, sweetheart. Very few people get opportunities like this."

She wasn't hearing me. She got my father on the phone, who repeated that I'd never get another opportunity like this and I should take it and see the world. That he would have killed for this gig if it had been offered to him.

But it hadn't. It had been offered to me.

Dad gave the phone back to Mom. "So what about coming up here to take Peter to dinner?" I asked.

"Oh, sweetheart, we can do that if you like. But long-distance relationships never work. Do you expect to stay with Peter while you travel Europe?"

Clearly not, her tone said.

"It would mean a lot to me."

"Logan. You're so young. Your life isn't set now. There will be other boys after Peter. There may never be another European tour. I know it's hard to see past the end of this semester, but really think about the long term, okay? Think about what's best for your career."

Did she even hear me?

"Mom, I—"

"I'm just saying. Everything feels important now, but a lot of it isn't. You'll lose touch with people you're friends with now. In twenty years, you won't even remember Peter's name."

My heart sank. Not because I thought she was right, but because she didn't get what I was saying. Talking to her was like talking to a wall.

I managed to get her off the phone, but I was no closer to deciding what to do.

I sat on my bed and pressed my face into my hands. I remembered suddenly the conversation I'd had with Noel a few weeks ago, when he'd told me about his doubts with Dave. Noel had chosen a risky path, but one that made him happier than the safer path would have. How could I relate that to my own life? Being a concert violinist wasn't a safe choice, exactly, but it was the predictable, expected path for a kid who had been training to be a violinist since before he could read. It was the same for Peter in a lot of ways; accounting was safe, expected. But maybe what we both needed was to shake things up, to leave the safe, expected path and try something risky but ultimately more fulfilling. I wasn't sure about Peter, but I knew for myself that there was something very appealing about the unknown, especially in the face of a known future I wasn't sure I even wanted. But it wouldn't be worth risking anything if Peter wasn't there with me.

CHAPTER 21

I DIDN'T bring up the topic with Peter until the next day, and I almost didn't then. But I was in our room, doing homework at my desk, when he got back from class—one of my extra rehearsals was finished for the rest of the semester now that the concert had passed—so I caught him at an unusual moment.

He nodded at me as he walked into the room and put his backpack on his desk. "Well, that was unpleasant."

"Class?"

"Yeah. This tax class is killing me. A few of the people in my class are making a study group for the final, so I think I'm going to join it. It's so hard to even make myself study this stuff. It's so boring it doesn't stick in my brain."

I nodded, although in all honesty, my mind was still on the European orchestra tour question. It felt like too good an opportunity to pass up, and I didn't have a real reason for turning it down, at least not one that I thought my parents and Costner would find persuasive. Peter was a factor, definitely. We'd come to mean a lot to each other in just a few weeks, and I couldn't just throw that away. School was a factor too, but my mother was probably right about that; whether or not I finished the BFA wouldn't have much of an impact on whether I'd be accepted to an orchestra. Whether I could play well was more important. And I *could* play. But was that what I wanted? Touring Europe had the potential to be really incredible. Would I be making a terrible mistake if I stayed in Massachusetts with Peter?

I must have made a sound, because Peter said, "Is everything all right?"

"What makes you ask?" The question came out shakily.

"You've been a little off since yesterday. Something seems wrong. Or not. Tell me to bug off if you want to."

"No." I felt like I was losing it. I just had no idea what to do or what I wanted or what was best or what I should do.

Peter sat on my bed and patted the space next to him. As I stood, I said, "I have to make a decision I don't know how to make. I have a couple of weeks to think about it, but I don't know how time will help, because it's *all* I can think about." I sat next to him but didn't touch him because I was worried about how he'd react.

We'd just started to make things work between us. I didn't want him to think I was ready to abandon him so soon.

"What is it?" he asked.

"I've been offered a spot in an orchestra that will tour Europe."

Peter's face broke into a huge smile. "Oh my God! That's amazing. Congratulations!"

"I'd have to leave in February."

The full picture of what I was saying seemed to dawn on him then. "Oh."

"And I can't decide what to do, because this is such an amazing opportunity, and it's exactly the kind of thing I've been working toward since I was five years old. I'll probably never get another opportunity like this."

"You don't sound happy about it."

"What about school? What about you?"

He nodded slowly. "Well, to start with, I care about you a great deal. You know that. And I just assumed I'd be spending the next semester with you too. But I don't want to stand in the way of your success. If you go overseas for a few months, I'll wait for you."

"It might be a year. Or longer."

"Longer?"

"This guy from the production company that runs the tour seems to think this is my ticket into a European orchestra."

"Oh." Peter's whole face fell.

"And I couldn't ask you to wait for me that long. Long distance never works, let alone across an ocean, and you deserve better than that."

"So you're going?"

"I don't know." I flopped back on the bed so that I lay with my head near the wall and my feet on the floor. I looked up at him. "According to everyone else, I don't have a good reason not to go. My mom thinks I should take the spot. So does Costner. I want to finish my degree, but it's not like a BFA will affect whether or not I can play a B-flat. As everyone keeps pointing out."

Peter looked down at me. Our gazes met for an instant. I suspected he could hear how I felt in my voice. "Okay. But what is it *you* want? Forget about your parents for a second. What do you, Logan, want from your life? Because at the end of the day, you're an adult. It's not your parents' life to live. It's yours."

Thinking about what he said earlier about his tax class, I said, "You should hear yourself talk."

I hated myself as soon as I said it. It sounded petty. But he and I were the same in a lot of ways, and surely he could see how hard this was.

I realized then that I loved him. That somehow, over the course of this semester, he'd gone from my adversary to my friend to my boyfriend to the most important person in my life. That my vision of the house in the Berkshires included him and not just some generic guy. That there wasn't a single other person in my life, not even Ellie, whom I could have this conversation with. That somehow I'd fallen completely, stupidly, amazingly in love with Peter.

He sighed and looked away. "Well, yeah, I know a thing or two about doing what your parents want when it's not what you want. But… I mean, I only have three semesters left."

"And then what? You take the CPA exam and slave away for your parents?"

He crossed his arms. "Or I work for my dad while I save up enough money to pay for art school on my own."

That took the wind out of my sails. We'd talked about it in the abstract, but I realized in that moment that he'd actually thought about how to parlay his present predicament into a real plan. I hadn't really gotten beyond staying at WMU versus Europe.

"I mean, the Europe trip is a good opportunity…," I said.

"Sure. But is it what you want?"

I wanted to shout that what I wanted was Peter. But that wasn't really what he was asking. I knew, though, that if I went to my parents and said I wanted to stay behind, they'd assume it was because of Peter. And it was, but it was also about me not wanting to spend the rest of my life playing in orchestras. It was about me doing something for myself instead of for my parents. It was about carving out the life that was the best fit for me, not the best fit for everyone else. It was about choosing the path that was risky but also rewarding and wonderful, instead of the path that was predictable, expected, and unsatisfying.

I knew the answer to Peter's question then. "I want to stay."

He looked down at me. "Are you sure?"

I sat up. I could feel how odd my hair had gotten, likely sticking out in every direction, and the blood rushed out of my head suddenly, but I took a deep breath and looked at him. "I don't want to go to Europe. I feel sick whenever I think about it. I don't want the life I've been training for."

Our gazes met and I was struck again by how much I loved him, how beautiful he was, how well he understood me. His sand-colored eyelashes were long, something I could only really see when I was this close to him. His eyes were the most amazing blue. Just looking at his face made my insides warm. He reached over to me and ran his hand along my arm. "There's your answer," he said softly.

"I want to stay with you too. I know you don't want that to be a factor, but it is. We just figured things out. I want to give us a chance to keep going. I don't want to leave you. Not yet. Maybe not ever."

He smiled. He took my hand. "Selfishly, I'm glad. But you should be happy too. Do what makes you happy."

"What would make me happy is staying here with you and finishing my degree and then figuring out what I want to do next, because touring Europe with an orchestra isn't it." It sounded insane to say it out loud. I looked around the room, at all my stuff and Peter's, at our books, his movie posters, his orange-and-purple sheets, my laptop, stray pieces of music paper, the strap of my violin case. Somehow a little envelope that had once contained a new E-string was under his desk. One of his books, a novel I'd borrowed, was on my desk. Our stuff was starting to intermingle the way our bodies often did at night.

I sighed. "Is it crazy not to want to go to Europe? Because I feel like that's what I should want."

Peter put his arm around me. "You want what you want."

"I want a quiet life."

"There's nothing wrong with that."

I put my head on his shoulder. I wanted to tell him I loved him, but I wasn't sure he returned the sentiment, and I didn't want to risk my heart. If he didn't feel the same, I didn't think I could bear it. I already felt vulnerable enough.

"Sleep on it," Peter said. "I'm here for you no matter what, though, okay? No matter what you decide. I'm here."

I put my arms around him and hugged him close. "Thank you." But my mind was made up. Now I just had to figure out how to tell everyone.

CHAPTER 22

I DROVE home that weekend. I spent half the trip thinking about where "home" really was. Was home my parents' house? Was it my dorm room? Neither felt quite right. The house I grew up in didn't feel like the refuge it had been when I'd been young. I'd always thought they'd been supportive, but the more time I spent away, the more I realized how they'd manipulated me. Maybe it wasn't conscious, but I'd been pushed and prodded into a box I didn't fit inside.

Maybe *manipulated* was too strong a word. They meant well. I was certain they were doing what they thought was best. But somewhere what I really wanted had gotten lost. I'd gone along with the program, because why wouldn't I want to become a concert violinist?

I felt frustrated. My mother hadn't heard anything I'd said in months, but I needed her to hear me now. Because I wasn't going to Europe. And if that meant I'd never get another opportunity to play with a professional orchestra, I was okay with that. There were regional and community orchestras. Playing with them would be less stressful. I could teach lessons to pay my way through grad school, maybe. Get a teaching degree, conduct a high school orchestra. That sounded pretty great. I'd come home to Peter and our dogs. I'd tell Peter I loved him every damn day.

Peter, who was back in our building at WMU. Of course, the dorm wasn't home either. It was a room we lived in temporarily. I'd have to move out at the end of the spring semester. And then what? Maybe Peter and I could get a place off campus. Were we ready for that? Was I jumping the gun? Did he even want to live in a house up in the mountains with me? What were his dreams, besides art school? Was I pushing this ahead too fast?

I pulled into the driveway at my parents' house and banged my head against the steering wheel. It didn't make me feel better, and now I had a headache.

I'd asked my parents to both be home, and they were in the living room watching TV—an opera on PBS, of fucking course—when I walked in the front door.

"Hi, sweetheart," my mother said.

They weren't bad parents. I knew they loved me. I'd never wanted for anything. While not wildly wealthy, we lived comfortably, and we always had good meals on the table and plenty of clothing to combat the finicky Massachusetts weather. They'd bought me three violins, and years' worth of lessons, and clothes for performances. And I'd enjoyed all of those things because I genuinely loved playing the violin. But no one had ever stopped to ask me what I wanted to do with my life, and it wasn't until I'd gotten away from home that I'd realized the life that had been laid out for me wasn't what I wanted.

I imagined that was true for Peter as well. How many years had gone by in which he just assumed his future would involve sitting beside his father during tax season doing… whatever accountants did? On the other hand, Peter's love of musical theater and the arts went back further than my nascent desire to have a more humble life, so maybe he'd been plotting his escape for a while. But I had to focus on what I planned to say now, so I pushed that aside.

My father flipped off the television. The scene reminded me of when I'd come out to them. Knowing they loved me had made that relatively easy. My stomach had churned then as it did now, but I'd had faith that I'd be all right in the end. My parents loved me, they'd never throw me out or cause me harm. I just hated to disappoint them. I'd done it once when I'd told them I was gay. Well, maybe not disappointed them, but changed their vision of me and how I'd live my life.

That's all this was now, I told myself. I was… changing their perception of me.

"Do you want something to eat?" Dad asked.

"No, I'm okay. I ate before I left school. I just really need to talk to you about something."

"Of course," said Mom.

I sat in the big armchair. I'd napped in this chair hundreds of times as a kid, here in this very living room, in a space that had always felt warm and friendly. I was lucky, really. My parents loved each other still. They loved me. They'd given me a good home.

I took a deep breath.

"Let me just say all this before you say anything," I said.

Mom and Dad exchanged a look. Dad nodded.

"Okay. So, I love the violin. I do. But my life to this point has been about 95 percent violin. Because, the thing is, I'm not a prodigy."

They both started to protest. I held up my hands. They quieted.

"I'm *not* a prodigy. I'm very good because I work hard at it, but I don't have the natural talent some other musicians have. And I'm okay with that. I'm not always sure you are."

"Darling," my mother said.

"Just listen, okay? Because I'm not a prodigy, in order to be good, I have to practice all the time. And what that has ended up meaning is that I don't have a life outside of my violin. Did you know that? Until this semester, I only had a couple of friends, and they were almost all in the orchestra. I went to a couple of parties freshman year, but you guys said that kind of thing was a distraction, so I stopped. My only extracurricular activity was playing violin in other ensembles. Do you know how lonely that gets? All around me, all these other kids were having fun, living their lives, meeting the people they're going to end up with. Kids at WMU go to parties and play sports and spend their Friday nights out at bars or the movies. I never do any of those things."

My mother reached for me, but I held up my hand again.

"I don't… I don't think it's worth it." Tears sprung to my eyes. "I'm tired, you know that? I'm so tired. I've worked so hard to get this spot in an orchestra, but for what? To sacrifice the entire rest of my life? I don't even think it's what I want anymore. Every time I think about Europe, I feel like I have to vomit. I'd like to visit Europe someday, but right now? I want to finish my bachelor's degree. Then I want to go to grad school for education. I want to get a teaching job. I want to teach kids how to play the violin and play in a community orchestra and have a full, rich life. I want to have friends and get married and be home enough to take care of a dog." By the time I finished talking, I was basically crying.

My parents exchanged looks again. My mother asked, "Is this about Pe—"

"It's not about Peter!" I took a deep breath to calm down, realizing I had yelled. "I've been feeling this way since before I even met him. But being with him this semester has just highlighted for me how much my life was passing me by while I was in rehearsal. Will I end up with Peter? I have no idea. But I deserve the chance to find out. I don't want to be forty and have nothing to show for it besides a chair in an orchestra."

"What are you telling us, son?" asked Dad.

I wiped my eyes and tried to get my emotions back under control. "I've decided not to accept the offer to tour Europe. I haven't told Professor Costner and Mr. Lundberg yet, but I will on Monday. I want to stay at WMU and finish my degree. And then we'll see, okay?"

My mother leaned forward. "I had no idea you felt this way."

"That's because you haven't listened to me. I've been trying to tell you all semester."

My mother let out a breath. She must have been going back over everything I said to her. She nodded slowly. "I guess you have. Oh, sweetheart. We just want you to be happy. You know that."

"I don't think playing with an orchestra in Europe would make me happy."

"Then don't take it. I'm sure Professor Costner would be thrilled to work with you for another year."

"Yeah. I'll have to talk to him too. I don't want extra rehearsals next year. I don't care if playing in an ensemble undermines his teaching or whatever. I want to play with the Theater Club pit orchestra again."

"Okay," said my father. "It's your decision. But!" He held up his hand. "If you stay at school, you have to keep your grades up. I'm not paying for you to party all the time."

"I will. I've made Dean's List every semester that I've been in school. I won't change that. Okay? I'll work hard, but I want to have fun too. Before I have to join the real world. You know?"

My father smiled, which surprised me. He reached over and patted my knee. "I remember what it was like to be your age. I understand."

And apparently we were done talking, because next thing I knew, my mother had wrapped her arms around me and was holding me tight. She stroked my hair.

"We love you, Logan. You know that. If I'd had any idea you were this unhappy, I wouldn't have put so much pressure on you. I just wanted you to succeed. I thought the orchestra was what you wanted."

"I did too for a long time. But it's not," I said, and then I really began to cry, mostly out of relief. Everything would be okay, I realized.

Mom helped me up. I wiped my eyes as I stood. My dad hugged me too. Then he said, "Are you sure we can't take you to dinner before we send you back to school? You can tell us more about this fellow of yours. Peter. He sounds like a special guy."

"He is, Dad. And, yeah. I can stay for dinner."

CHAPTER 23

I DROVE back to campus late that night. For some reason I thought Peter would be out. It was a Saturday night, after all. Maybe he'd gone out with the QSU kids, or was hanging out with Dave or Lily or one of his hundreds of other friends. I felt a pang of something like jealousy or regret. He was so greatly loved and I was such a grouch. Had I been holding him back? Was he out having fun without me?

I reached peak self-loathing as I rode the elevator up to my floor. Then I was startled to find Peter was home, sitting at his desk, leaning over a textbook.

He turned around when I closed the door behind me. "Hey," he said. "How did it go?"

I tossed my keys on my desk. "Not bad, actually. We had a good talk. I'm not going to Europe." I looked around. All the lights were on, as was Peter's clunky old laptop, though it was shoved to the side. He had a notebook open next to the textbook. "I'm surprised you're here. I figured you'd go out tonight."

He shrugged. "Everyone was busy. Dave and Noel are both working. Lily went home for the weekend. Maggie and her boyfriend are out on some anniversary dinner. And so on. I have a ton of tax homework due Monday too." He put his pen down and looked at his notes before looking back up to me. "Plus I wanted to stick around and see how things went for you."

That touched me. I felt emotionally fragile and confused and was worried he'd make me cry again. I swallowed. "Well, um. I guess I just needed to tell my parents directly what I was really thinking."

He nodded. "That's a good policy generally, don't you think?"

It occurred to me then that I'd never told Peter exactly how I felt. That I was too worried he didn't love me back to tell him

I loved him. But the lesson I'd learned this semester was that it was always better to just say what was important, to not make any assumptions. I'd just laid it all out for my parents, and things were going to change. So I should lay it all out for Peter too.

But I asked, "Would you have rather have gone out instead of waiting here for me all night?"

He shrugged again. "In a perfect world, I would have gone out with you."

There was that.

I felt stuck, standing next to my desk as if my feet were suddenly cement. I didn't know what to do or say. On the one hand, a laxer rehearsal schedule meant I *would* be able to go out with Peter more next semester, at which time we could spend more time together and see how things went. Except I knew how I wanted things to go. How did he feel? Why couldn't I just say how I felt without waiting for him? Was he waiting for me?

Good Lord, what was wrong with me?

Peter stood. "You look like you need a hug."

"It *has* been a hard day."

He took a step to close the distance between us and pulled me into a hug. I relaxed into him. His scent was familiar now, comforting. He was wearing a fleece pullover that was soft against me. I put my arms around him and leaned my face against his shoulder, and I hugged him with everything I had.

"Can I ask you something?" I asked.

"Sure."

"You seem to have a plan for after college. Become a CPA, work for your father, save money, art school."

"It's a possible plan."

"What does that mean?"

He stepped back and took my hand. He led me over to his bed, where we sat side by side. "Maybe you've inspired me. Maybe it's time to have a long overdue talk with my parents. I mean, I'll probably finish the accounting degree, and it might be a good idea to get a job doing tax prep or something to help pay for art school, but I don't know. Maybe if I'm clear with my parents about what my hopes and dreams really are, they'll be understanding. Your parents were, right?"

"Yeah. More than I expected them to be."

"I can't see my father being happy with me not finishing my accounting degree or with me wanting to go to art school. He's not thrilled that I'm gay and gives me a hard time about it sometimes. When I was in high school, he called my interest in art girly. But the older I get, the more I realize that I have to live my life for me and not for my father. He's paying for school now, so I'll finish here, but after that, I'll be on my own and can make different choices."

"So you'd choose art school. What else?"

"What do you mean?"

I took his hand and curled my fingers around his. "I don't ever want you to feel like I'm holding you back, and I don't want to impose my vision of the future on you. I want to know what you hope and dream. Beyond school. Say you're an artist or a designer or you're designing sets for Broadway. Where would you live?"

"I don't know. I suppose I could live anywhere. I kind of like it out here, actually. Away from the city. You know?"

"I do know."

"Is this your roundabout way of asking me if you fit into my future somewhere?"

I met his gaze. "Maybe."

"I'm not picky about where I'll live after college. Who I live with is more important."

I looked away. "Peter, I…." But I trailed off, unable to finish the sentence.

"You what? What is it? You know you can tell me anything."

I did know that. I knew he'd be by my side through whichever life choices I made, because I was going to make choices that included him. I knew that if things had gone south with my parents today, he would have supported me. I knew that when he wanted to do social things, he wanted me to be with him. And I knew that if I wanted it, I'd have a place in his future plans.

I squeezed his hand. "I love you," I said. "I really do. I love you, and I want you to know that."

He put his fingers below my chin and lifted it until I met his gaze. He smiled. "Logan. I love you too. You have to know that."

I did. Somewhere deep down, I did. I knew that things would likely not always be smooth sailing for us, that there was a lot we'd have to deal with once we graduated, that there was still a lot of uncertainty in the future. But I also knew that I'd do everything I could to stay by his side. I'd support him just as I knew he'd support me. I'd love him fiercely through all of it. We'd figure it all out together.

I kissed him. He moaned softly into my mouth and cupped my cheek and kissed me back. We deepened the kiss, opening our mouths, licking into each other.

I didn't know what the future held, but for once, I was okay with that.

EPILOGUE

Three Years Later

IT WASN'T a cute little house in the Berkshires, but our home was a small two-bedroom ranch house a few miles north of the WMU campus. Peter and I were renting it together while we finished grad school. I liked the house, but I often fantasized about what I'd do with it if I owned it; I'd choose different paint colors and add built-in bookshelves to the living room and remodel the kitchen to use the space more efficiently. I'd probably been watching too much HGTV in my downtime, but I had a lot of ideas for what I could do with this space, or any space I ended up living in. Now that Peter and I were both close to finishing our master's degrees, I figured we'd buy a house together once we had steady jobs, and then we could do whatever we wanted with it.

This semester, I was student teaching at the local high school and working as an assistant orchestra director. It was hard work, and sometimes I struggled to relate to the kids, but I often had a sense when I was at school that this was the work I was meant to do. It was early in the semester, so I supposed odds were I'd be disillusioned by the end of it. But right now it was perfect.

I'd also set up a little business for myself teaching private lessons, though a lot of my students were adults. I felt awkward sometimes teaching people who were much older than I was how to play simple songs, but it was rewarding too, especially when my students showed real progress. And it earned me enough money to afford half the rent on our little house.

We'd been talking about what we'd do after we finished grad school, about where we'd move, what breed of dog we'd get when we lived somewhere that would allow pets, what kinds of jobs

Peter would look for. We'd talked everyday things like whether we should buy property and if we should have a joint bank account to pay for household stuff.

It was all very practical, but I could still see that perfect vision of the future. Peter and I had gone up to Vermont for a vacation the previous summer, and on the drive home, we'd passed this gorgeous house up near Lenox that I could totally imagine us living in. Ever since, I'd concocted this elaborate fantasy in which Peter and I lived in that house with two dogs and a baby and we were just blissfully happy.

But first, I had to get home. That afternoon, there was a blizzard, swirls of snowflakes falling fast as I left school. I drove carefully, but the snow was starting to come down pretty hard. The main roads were clear, but when I turned onto our street, the going became much more difficult. I'd lived in Massachusetts my whole life, so I had good instincts for driving in bad weather, and even though my car was not the sturdiest, it had good tires, so I made it to our house in one piece.

Peter was home when I got there. He stuck his head out from the second bedroom when I walked in the door. We'd converted the bedroom to a studio/practice room, so I guessed he'd been painting.

"Thank goodness you're home," he said. "I saw the snow starting to come down and worried."

"Early dismissal at school. I think if school had let out on time, I'd be sleeping there tonight."

Peter crossed the living room and hugged me before I was even all the way out of my snowy coat.

I gently nudged him away so I could properly get out of my wet clothes. "What was that about?"

"I've just been worried since the snow started really falling. I didn't want to text you in case you were on the road. So I'm glad you made it home unharmed."

I put my arms around him. "I did. And I was thinking, since it looks like we'll be snowed in for a day or two, maybe tonight we could find a movie to stream and get under the blankets on the couch and drink hot chocolate."

He smiled. "That sounds perfect. Oh, but first I have a question for you. Come with me."

I followed him back into the studio. He definitely had been painting when I'd walked in; his painting stuff was spread all over his worktable, and it smelled like the oil paints he liked to use. He was very strict about putting everything away when he wasn't using it. On his easel he had a canvas up that was an incredible burst of color. It seemed to be abstract, perhaps intended to convey an emotion more than a physical object. It was beautiful and vibrant, a sunburst of yellows and oranges, and I loved it, and I loved him so much I sometimes thought my heart would burst.

"Well, two questions, I guess," he said. "First, what do you think of this?" He gestured toward the canvas. "Professor Farber wants me to play around with abstract concepts more, so I'm trying to use color to show joy."

"It's gorgeous. I can definitely see the joy."

"Most of the other students in my studio are all angsty and sad all the time." Peter bent below his desk and started rummaging through a drawer. "Kind of like you when we first met, actually."

"Ha-ha."

He chuckled. "But, you know, everyone thinks they have to have a lot of inner turmoil in order to be a good artist. I guess I'm trying to prove you can be happy and produce good art. That talent and discipline matter more. I mean, I'm finally doing what I want to do and I have a great boyfriend, so what is there not to be happy about? Geez, where the heck did I put…."

His voice became muffled as he started tossing things around and digging into his desk. I decided to leave him to it and focus on his canvas. I tried to see how he experienced joy, if it was like a burst or explosion, if it was all about bright colors. "This is very good." I looked closely. He'd used wide brushstrokes, which wasn't his usual style, but I could see where he was trying to convey something specific. "I like how pure it is, with the long lines here, and the colors. There's a lot of joy here."

"That's good. I'm glad. That, uh, leads me to my second question." He stood back up. "I was going to wait to ask this, but honestly, I've been holding on to this for a while, and I don't want to wait anymore. Because I realized while I was waiting for you to come home that if your car had spun out on the highway and you'd been in some terrible accident, my life would have been over. Because somehow, even though you still have a stick up your ass most of the time, I love you more than I ever thought possible and you're the most important person in my life."

"I love you too, Peter."

He nodded. "So I bought this for you for our anniversary last year, but then I chickened out and didn't give it to you. But I want to give it to you now. Because we belong together, Logan. I want to be with you for the rest of my life, if you'll have me."

My heart stopped and I stared at him. I realized quite suddenly that he held something small in his hand. He held it out to me. It was a little jewelry box. I took it slowly, willing my heart and my breathing to resume their normal functions but so shocked I was unable to do it.

Peter stepped closer and held my shoulders. "I love you, Logan. Will you marry me?"

My mouth wouldn't form words. I looked at him for a long time, meeting his gaze and seeing his complete sincerity. I looked down at the jewelry box in my hand and opened it. There were two simple silver bands there. Not expensive, probably—he was an art student, after all—but completely heartfelt. Priceless, in other words.

Tears sprung to my eyes. "Yes," I said. "Of course. Yes."

He kissed me in that startling way he had, a hard kiss that robbed me of my senses, and then he took the box and slipped one of the rings onto my finger and the other onto his own. "I figure, you know, when we get married, we can get better rings. These are really just placeholders until we make it official. But I wanted to do something."

"These are perfect."

I put my arms around him and he hugged me back, and we stayed that way for a long time, standing next to his painting of joy, with the snow falling outside the studio window. I closed my eyes and rested my head on his shoulder.

"This is not how I pictured my life turning out when I met you," I said.

"No?"

"This is a million times better."

KATE MCMURRAY writes smart romantic fiction. She likes creating stories that are brainy, funny, and, of course, sexy with regular-guy characters and urban sensibilities. She advocates for romance stories by and for everyone. When she's not writing, she edits textbooks, watches baseball, plays violin, crafts things out of yarn, and wears a lot of cute dresses. She's active in Romance Writers of America, serving for two years on the board of Rainbow Romance Writers, the LGBT romance chapter, and three—including two as president—on the board of the New York City chapter. She lives in Brooklyn, NY, with two cats and too many books.

Website: www.katemcmurray.com
Twitter: @katemcmwriter
Facebook: www.facebook.com/katemcmurraywriter

THERE HAS
TO BE A
REASON

KATE McMURRAY

WMU: Book One

Dave is enjoying his junior year at a big New England university, even if none of his relationships have been especially satisfying. He plans to hang around with his best friend Joe and focus on his studies until he graduates, and then he'll figure out the rest.

Meeting Noel changes his plans.

Noel is strikingly beautiful and unlike anyone Dave knows. Something about Noel draws Dave to him—an attraction Dave doesn't feel ready to label. And even if he was, why would Noel be interested in Dave? And what about Joe? He hates Noel and everything he represents, and he might hate Dave if he finds out about Dave's secret desires. So Dave will have to keep those feelings hidden—along with his relationship with Noel.

But Noel has fought too hard for his identity to be Dave's dirty secret. Will Dave tell the truth and risk the life he's always known… or live a lie and risk losing the love of his life?

www.dreamspinnerpress.com

THE

BOY

NEXT

DOOR

KATE McMURRAY

Life is full of surprises and, with luck, second chances.

After his father's death, Lowell leaves the big city to help his sick mother in the conservative small town where he grew up. He's shocked to find himself living next to none other than his childhood friend Jase. Lowell always had a crush on Jase, and the man has only gotten more attractive with age. Unfortunately Jase is straight, now divorced, and raising his six-year-old daughter. It's nice to reconnect, but Lowell doesn't see a chance for anything beyond friendship.

Until a night out together changes everything.

Jase can't fight his growing feelings for Lowell, and he doesn't want to give up the happy future they could have. But his ex-wife issues an ultimatum: he must keep his homosexuality secret or she'll revoke his custody of their daughter, Layla. Now Jase faces an impossible choice: Lowell and the love he's always wanted, or his daughter.

www.dreamspinnerpress.com

KATE McMURRAY
DEVIN
DECEMBER

A freak blizzard strands flight attendant Andy Weston at LaGuardia Airport on Thanksgiving. Tabloid reports about Hollywood It couple Devin Delaney and Cristina Marino breaking up in spectacular fashion keep Andy sane. And then Devin Delaney himself turns up at the gate Andy is working. Against all odds—and because there's nothing else to do—Andy and Devin begin to talk, immediately connect, and, after Devin confesses the real reason he broke up with Cristina, have a magical night together snowed in at the airport. But the magic ends when Devin boards his flight home the next morning, and Andy assumes it's over.

Then Devin turns up on his doorstep. Andy is game for a clandestine affair at first—who could turn down one of the hottest men on the planet? But he soon grows tired of being shoved in Devin's closet. As Christmas approaches, it's clear that this will never work unless Devin is willing to make some big changes. Devin has a holiday surprise in store—but will it be enough?

www.dreamspinnerpress.com

DREAMSPUN DESIRES

THE GREEK TYCOON'S GREEN CARD GROOM

Kate McMurray

Marriage gets less convenient when love is involved.

Marriage gets less convenient when love is involved.

It started simple: Ondrej Kovac marries Archie Katsaros so Ondrej can stay in the US, away from his judgmental family in eastern Europe. Archie marries Ondrej in exchange for the money to bail out his failing company. It's a fraud neither man is convinced he can pull off.

But as Archie introduces Ondrej to New York society and Ondrej proves his skill in the office, they start to discover a connection between them. Can they overcome the rocky foundation their relationship was built on, meddling immigration agents, gossip columnists determined to out their deception, and an aggressive executive set on selling Archie's company out from under him? Only if they can prove to each other their love is worth fighting for.

www.dreamspinnerpress.com

KATE McMURRAY

OUT
IN THE
FIELD

Matt Blanco is a legend on the Brooklyn Eagles, but time and injuries have taken their toll. With his career nearing its end, he's almost made it to retirement without anyone learning his biggest secret: he's gay in a profession not particularly known for its tolerance.

Iggy Rodriquez is the hot new rookie in town, landing a position in the starting lineup of the team of his dreams and playing alongside his idol, Matt Blanco. Iggy doesn't think it can get any better, until an unexpected encounter in the locker room with Matt proves him wrong.

A relationship—and everything it could reveal—has never been in the cards for Matt, but Iggy has him rethinking his priorities. They fall hard for each other, struggling to make it through trades, endorsement deals, and the threat of retirement. Ultimately they will be faced with a choice: love or baseball?

www.dreamspinnerpress.com

The
WINDUP

KATE McMURRAY

THE RAINBOW LEAGUE

The Rainbow League: Book One

Ian ran screaming from New York City upon graduating from high school. A job offer too good to turn down has brought him back, but he plans to leave as soon as the job is up. In the meantime he lets an old friend talk him into joining the Rainbow League, New York's LGBT amateur baseball league. Baseball turns out to be a great outlet for his anxiety, and not only because sexy teammate Ty has caught his eye.

Ty is like a duck on a pond—calm and laid-back on the surface, a churning mess underneath. In Ian, he's found someone with whom he feels comfortable enough to share some of what's going on beneath the surface. The only catch is that Ian is dead set on leaving the city as soon as he can. Ty works up a plan to convince Ian that New York is, in fact, the greatest city in the world. But when Ian receives an offer for a job overseas, Ty needs a new plan: convince Ian that home is where Ty is.

www.dreamspinnerpress.com